A DOCTOR
COMES
TO BAYARD

Elizabeth Seifert

A DELL BOOK

Published by DELL PUBLISHING CO., INC.
750 Third Avenue, New York, N.Y. 10017

Reprinted by arrangement with
Dodd, Mead & Company, New York, N.Y.

DEDICATION: For the Smiths

First Dell Printing—October, 1965

Printed in U.S.A.

Chapter 1

IT WAS LIKE A BALLET, THOUGHT DEWEY WINDSOR. The hands of the doctors, of the instrument nurse—even his own hand on the valves and switches of the anesthesia apparatus. The lights from overhead, and the shadows they cast, were more dramatic than he had ever seen on the stage of any theater. The glint upon the instruments, the high lights upon gloves and drapes, towels and sponges, and always the hands, in and out, precise exact and delicate. An instrument slapped into a curved palm which lifted it, balanced it into position, and thrust forward to use it.

He let himself look up at the surgeon's face and at the assistant's. Gauze-masked, down-bent, they were like the intent faces of puppeteers; their puppets were their hands.

Alison Cornel, the surgeon, was a very big man; so was his assistant, Garde Shelton. And yet no ballerina could move with more grace than did their gloved fingers, lightly, exquisitely, every gesture meaningful and to a purpose.

Sometime, Dewey thought, he would bring a camera in here and try to get the colors, the play of light and shadow —the motion of those hands, lifted, awaiting the next instrument, clasping it, using it, casting it aside, lifted again.

The doctor sighed and looked again at his gauges.

"I live for the day when we can have a proper anesthetist," he said, when he could push the mask down from his face, the tight cap up from his forehead.

"You're doing all right."

"I make myself do all right. But—we need an anesthetist, Cornel."

The surgeon mumbled something, and Dewey ambled off to check on the patient before changing into whites for the

5

rest of his day's work.

Dr. Cornel's orders written, the patient checked on by him, he came into the doctors' room and, as he opened his locker door, he quoted Dewey.

"We have a threatened strike here, Shelton," he commented.

"I can see his point," Garde Shelton answered, his deep voice echoing against the tiles of the shower stall. "Dewey is an internist. He must need to do a lot of studying in anesthesia. And he can't serve both masters well."

Dr. Cornel chuckled and glanced at Dewey Windsor, whose cheeks had reddened, but he made a gesture of surrender. "I do my best," he said comically.

Dr. Ruble came in, still wearing street clothes, and the other doctors rallied him about his late hours and freedom from o.r. responsibilities.

"When I am next called out at three A.M., I'll give you chaps a ring," the obstetrician promised. "How'd the resection go?"

"Fine for everybody but Windsor," said Dr. Shelton, sitting down to put on his shoes. "Get me a cup of coffee while you're at it, Bob. Please?"

"Glad to. When do you leave for the city, Dewey?" Bob Ruble asked over his shoulder.

Dewey glanced at the clock. "I have rounds—and some office appointments. I thought about eleven."

"Hazel going with you?"

Dr. Windsor looked surprised. "No. Why should she?"

"Well—" Bob Ruble glanced at the other men, who were nodding. "When I go to the city, I am usually well-chaperoned."

"My wife trusts me," said Dr. Windsor pompously, and the men laughed.

"My chaperone always carries a shopping list," said Alison Cornel, "and the shops out near the medical school are mur-der!"

"Obviously," said Dewey, getting his coffee cup, "I have my household under better control."

"You think."

Dewey shrugged. "I think," he agreed, and sat down on the couch as if he expected to lounge there all day.

He mentioned his project of taking a movie of the doctors' hands during surgery; he elaborated upon the colors—green robes, red rubber gloves, chrome steel, a square of white gauze . . .

"Red blood," drawled Garde Shelton, "not to mention—"

"Then don't mention it!" said Dewey sharply.

The men sat silent for a minute, relaxing, summoning strength for the day which lay ahead. This was a busy hospital and clinic.

Dr. Cornel spoke of the substitutions which might be necessary with their internist gone all afternoon. "What time do you expect to get back?" he asked Dewey.

"Well, let me see," said Dewey, making an elaborate pretense of being conscientious over the time to be consumed on this trip which he was to make to the city to address the graduating and third-year medical students of the two big schools there. "I've checked this out with Hazel," he explained, "and we decided—"

"She did," said Bob Ruble, his eyes twinkling.

"Togetherness is the guiding light in the Windsor domicile."

"Ah-huh!"

Dewey nodded. "I'll leave here at eleven. There's a luncheon at one—"

"To tell you what to say."

"I'll explain that my cohorts in Bayard have already taken care of that item."

"But it is important, Dewey," said Dr. Cornel intently. "If you are to sell small-town practice—"

"I'll sell it."

"Don't go getting clever, will you?" Bob urged.

"I will if inspired," said Dewey hardily. "Though maybe one of you birds could do this better?"

"Oh, come off," said Garde. "You'll do a good job."

"You hope."

"Well . . ."

Bob Ruble went over to Dewey's locker. "Want to see what you'll be wearing," he explained. "I don't suppose you'll show up in those whites."

Dewey smoothed the duck across his thigh. "They have their own appeal," he murmured.

"Oh, you're wearing your Glen plaid," announced Bob. "Well, that will be all right."

"It brings out the blue in my eyes," said Dewey primly. "Pleatless trousers, hooked vent, and lapped seams. The plaid, you know, is called self-plaid."

"You are an idiot," growled Bob.

"I fancy that suit myself," Dewey admitted, standing up and reaching for his white jacket.

"Well, I thought I'd check. I didn't want you to be too handsome and risk your wife's happiness. I am very fond of Hazel."

"So am I," said Dr. Windsor. He glanced at Alison Cornel. "Unless I stay over to eat dinner, I'll be home by dark."

"Stay over, if you would spend the time finding that anesthesiologist."

"Well, now that is an idea!"

"And stay out till midnight if you'll bring back a radiologist, too," said Garde Shelton. "Full-time, experienced—"

"Both of them?" asked Dewey, picking up a pad of paper and a pencil.

"We do need them, you clown."

Dewey wrote things on the pad. "Young?" he asked seriously. "Old? Handsome? Not so . . ."

"Now, seriously," said Garde. Dewey glanced at him. Shelton was serious. "Do you think you could do it?"

"Bring one back *tonight*?"

"No, but get one spoken for."

Dewey tossed the memo pad and the pencil toward the table. "Seriously, Shelton," he said, and he too spoke seriously, "I'll bring one back—if it harelips the whole clinic."

He went out of the room. The other men looked at the door. "He'll do it, too," said Dr. Cornel.

"Get an anesthes . . . ?"

"Harelip the whole clinic."

"Dewey's all right."

"Dewey is fine. When his mind is on his profession. But when he is being funny—"

"He'll do his job today, Cornel. You know he will. And his breezy manner is just what will get those young medics."

Dr. Cornel nodded. "I suppose you're right."

Dr. Windsor did not get to leave the clinic before twelve, so he had to drive with a steady concentration on reaching the city, and threading through its traffic, in time to make the luncheon. He did make it, and there he met the other members of the panel. The president of the State Medical Society was the host; the subject of the afternoon's symposium was to be on out-state medical practice, and the participants, like Dewey Windsor, were doctors who practiced in communities away from the large medical and research centers.

During the meal the talk dealt mainly on personalities, and, Dewey decided, a good deal of boasting was in the air.

"Let me tell you what I was up against one night last week . . ." That preface was used many times.

Dr. Windsor told no stories; instead, he doodled on the tablecloth. Why didn't these birds save their experiences for the medics?

He was pleasant, he was friendly, and Cornel need not have worried; he had no inspiration to be funny.

At two the group moved from the staff dining room to the assembly hall where they would sit around three sides of a table on the platform. Eight men and the moderator, no one sitting with his back to the audience of medical students, interns, and some resident doctors.

Dewey, remembering the morning's discussion, noted the dress of his colleagues. Cornel would never have passed that red tie. And one man had two-toned shoes. Dewey clicked his tongue, saw the moderator glance his way, and he settled back into his chair. His eyes traveled around the hall. High, arched windows—the place obviously could be, and probably was, used for dances and so on. There were no frills . . .

The moderator was talking a bit too long about what the panel would say. Why didn't the man just let 'em say it?

The students sat in three blocks of chairs—sixty chairs to a block. Some of the men wore whites. In a semicircle embracing the seried blocks of chairs were other chairs—two or three rows of them—where sat older men and a few women; the hall was full.

Dewey should listen to what was being said so he wouldn't duplicate—not that he would. The panel members had been selected carefully. The boot-heel doctor in solo practice— the partnership man—a Public Health man—a representative of the nine-man clinic in the northern part of the state— a suburban doctor—and Dewey Windsor, of Bayard.

He watched the audience again. The students were listening respectfully enough. Some of the older ones—graduate physicians obviously—were more intent. Of the women— there were three girls among the students—one was pretty and knew it; one was quiet, listening; one was overly intent. Probably an eager beaver and unpopular. More than was usual unpopularity for a hen medic.

In the rows at the rear there were two women. One was very interested. The other . . . He straightened. It couldn't *be*! He craned his neck a little, then remembered where he was and relaxed. But that dark-haired woman in the last row certainly did look like . . . He couldn't see her clearly—somebody's head was always getting in the way. But that dark hair, the tilt of her chin—it certainly did look like . . .

The man next to him rose to speak his piece, and Dewey made himself listen, his finger tips tracing the scratches on the table before him.

Each panel member was supposed to answer three questions and then talk about his own situation with those answers in view. This bird, like all the others—and as Dewey would do in his turn—said that, yes, he liked out-state medical practice. What did the audience expect? That these M.D.'s had come in here to say they *didn't* like it?

Some didn't.

"Are you succeeding at it?" This chap was.

Some didn't.

"Can others do the same?" The man said yes.

And so they could.

This fellow was in private practice; he estimated the lowest possible cost of equipping a man's own office would be two thousand dollars. Which could be borrowed.

A man working alone pretty well had to be a general practitioner. But other specialities could band together like the nine-man clinic upstate and the four-man unit at Bayard.

Dewey glanced up at the speaker.

This chap worked alone. And his greatest problem was home obstetrics.

"On the kitchen table?" murmured Dewey, forgetting to watch himself.

The speaker glanced down at him. "Er—yes," he said. "If possible. Sometimes it is hard to get them off the bed and *on* the table. The family usually asks why the patient should be moved. Besides, the supper dishes didn't get cleared away that evening—"

"D'you wash them?" asked Dr. Windsor, and a ripple of laughter stirred the students.

"I have done it," said the speaker grimly, and the audience laughed again.

"But of course," the doctor continued, "I don't have to

worry too much about hospital staph for the mother or the baby. This advantage is somewhat counteracted by the poor illumination provided by coal-oil lamps. Then there is the unsolicited advice from grandmothers and elderly aunts who insist on attending the birth."

He glanced down at Dewey who had decided to shut up. He wasn't going to want heckling when his turn came.

The down-state doctor said that he now provided better lighting by rigging a wire from his automobile to a large lamp which he set up where needed indoors. And he had got rid of the grandmothers by buying four iron beds and setting them up in an improvised ward adjoining his office, a nearby restaurant contracting to furnish meals to his patients. For a couple of minutes longer he talked about the handicap which a lack of diagnostic and hospital facilities presented, but he concluded hopefully with the statement that progress was being made in hospital construction and he felt sure that the time was close when no community would be farther than fifty miles away from a hospital.

Dewey was the next, and last, speaker, and as he was introduced and stood up he had a mental picture of himself there on the platform. Thin as a bean stake, his brush-cut hair as white as snow, his skin as pink as a baby's. His self-plaid suit and pleatless trousers—a pixy grin crossed his face, and the audience stirred with interest.

"I am Dewey Windsor," he said firmly. "I am internist at the Bayard Hospital and Clinic, fifty miles north of here. I like the work I do and the place where I live. I make a better than adequate income, and I will say now that you birds couldn't do better than find a setup like my own.

"Maybe I should now sit down. But I'll go on and tell what I was sent down here to tell.

"In Bayard we have a hospital, completely modern—only fifteen years old—of forty beds, with three more beds for diagnostic observation. We have one o.r. and an emergency room and a delivery room, both of which can serve as o.r.'s.

We have a lab and x-ray facilities. We employ a part-time radiologist but could certainly use one full-time.

"Adjoining our hospital at the rear is our clinic building with offices and examination rooms for the doctors on the staff. It is very convenient for us doctors to have our out-patient offices so close to the hospital. We can, if necessary, dash across and look at a patient in hospital without disrupting our office hours, or using any gasoline, either.

"Our staff consists of four men, each certified in his specialty—a surgeon, Alison Cornel, who is our Chief of Staff, an o.b.-gyn man, Robert Ruble, and a pediatrician, Garde Shelton, who also has passed the surgery board. In the town there are a practicing physician and three D.O.'s, not affiliated with us. Ours is a privately owned hospital with a closed staff, though we do have as an associate the doctor who serves the big anhydrous-ammonia plant at Plover, ten miles away. He also is a certified surgeon, now at the age of semi-retirement. That means he hates to do rounds."

He was holding his audience comfortably in his hand. His smile was friendly; his china-blue eyes sparkled with enthusiasm.

"We have had, one time, a student-extern, and we hope to repeat that experience. It helped all concerned.

"Now I can see certain questions in your faces. Our oldest doctor is fifty, our youngest is forty.

"And, yes, we do get time off both for recreation and for study. Each man on the staff is forcibly encouraged to do at least one three-week clinic course every year, and provisions are made for him to attend shorter study programs. We come down here regularly for demonstrations and clinics.

"The town of Bayard is a pleasant one, some of it old, and a lot of it progressively new. The population is about fifteen thousand, with medical service given to as many as ten thousand other people in nearby towns and rural neighborhoods. From that many people we get a good spectrum of cases, and we care for them all. Measles to meningitis, skull fracture to gout. We don't attempt complicated neurosurgery or open-heart. We also wish we had an EET man on our staff and now refer such cases, except under emergency conditions.

"The advantages of service such as ours are many. Income and local prestige are good. We are close enough to the city to have cultural contacts available; the residents of the community are, many of them, like the doctors, educated people who enjoy the leisure afforded by semi-rural living. We do not feel the pressures which are known to city dwellers. Our families know each other, but our friends are not confined to our profession, which is good.

"Life in such a place puts obligations upon the doctors, of course. We feel it necessary and desirable to engage in civic work. Dr. Cornel, our chief surgeon, is on the school board; I am a member of the City Council, and we are all working church members.

"We are all, as well, members of the local fire department, which is largely a volunteer organization, but an efficient one. We are, too, members of the river patrol. Bayard is on the river, you know, and boating is our number-one recreation. We doctors each own a boat. Mine is the smallest. No, I take that back. Dr. Cornel's girls have a smaller one, a plastic job that is fun but not roomy. We—the men on the staff— are close friends, and we see to it that each of us keeps up on his medicine. That is perhaps our prime obligation.

"But life is pleasant for us. The wooded countryside is beautiful and within walking distance. On the streets we pass friends and acquaintances, not hurrying strangers. We know a serenity that a city dweller cannot even imagine.

"The river town is beautiful. Dr. Shelton lives in a tall, Mansard-roofed house over a hundred years old. I live in a pleasant clapboard one that is only twelve years old. Contemporary in style. My wife raises beautiful flowers and a fat cocker spaniel. Dr. Ruble lives in what was formerly a big red-brick farmhouse which he has modernized and added

14

to until it is a wonder of screened porches, flagstone patios, and boasts a fenced-in swimming pool. He has pasture land for three horses, and the woods are just beyond. Dr. Cornel lives in a handsome new Colonial house on the bluff overlooking the river, but he planned the thing himself, and there are three doors in the kitchen—one to the garage, one to the outdoors, and one to the pantry—that can't possibly be opened more than one at a time. He's a better surgeon than he is an architect.

"The sort of medicine we do . . ."

Dewey talked for another five minutes, his audience fascinated and ready to laugh when he let himself get just a little funny. Nothing Cornel could really object to, he told himself. The Bayard Hospital did get some pretty wacky situations and some really challenging ones as well.

The students were entranced. And so was the tall young woman in the back row. She was leaning forward, her chin on her fist, her lips parted over teeth that sparkled in the way Dewey well remembered.

He tried to talk to other corners of the room, to the redheaded man in the first row, to the pretty hen medic, to the wryly skeptical chap over to the left—that one would never be caught dead working anywhere but on the staff of a thousand-bed complex!—but in spite of all effort, Dewey's eyes kept returning to the handsome woman in the back of the hall, and he spoke directly to her.

"Now!" he concluded, looking down at the men in the first rows. "Are there any questions?"

There were. A dozen questions.

The moderator opened the meeting to questions, and sometimes lengthy answers by the men on the panel. There was one windy chap who had memorized every five-syllable word in the book!

Dewey jiggled impatiently and was glad when at four o'clock the moderator adjourned the meeting and the panel members were free to go down on the floor and talk individually with those who wanted to talk to them. Many did, milling about—nice, clean-cut chaps, interested as all get-out in what they would do with their medical lives. The least an established doctor could do was to talk to them with true interest. And patience.

But still it was a relief when finally, at long last, the crowd thinned, and the tall, handsome young woman was standing there, her hand outstretched. She was smiling.

Dewey stepped toward her, excitement racing his pulse, thickening his voice. "Libby!" he cried. "I couldn't believe my eyes!"

"It's been a long time." said the tall girl—and "girl" was right for Libby Gillis. The years had not touched her. She had always dressed well. Today she wore a black suit with something white folded in at the throat; her hair was glossy, and—well—it didn't look fussed with.

Dewey held her hand warmly in both of his and grinned at her. To go back—to his intern years—Libby had been in med school. There had been ways in which young Dr. Windsor could help Libby, and he had been glad to do it. He had liked Libby a lot! She was a grand person, ready to take her knocks with the men students, ready, too, to be a great girl on a date.

Dewey had used to think—he still thought—that he and Libby Gillis could have married. . . .

But, of course, all the time there was Hazel back in his home town; he and Hazel had been a "thing" since their college years. The two families were close friends and expected the young people to marry.

And when the young doctor was abruptly faced with war service he had, on a week's notice, married Hazel and gone off to camp with her, to England without her, and then, after the war, to a year or two for both of them in Austria.

That behind them, they had come to Bayard, and his work with the hospital and clinic had been good, his life with Hazel had been good.

Though now, at this particular minute, he was extremely glad to see Libby Gillis again. And she to see him. They said so in a dozen ways.

They were interrupted; they waited on each other, and talked again. The moderator came up and thanked Dr. Windsor.

"Are you staying over?"

"I'll go back later this evening . . ."

"Well, thank you very much."

"It was a privilege," said Dr. Windsor. He turned back to Libby. "Now. How about dinner? We have to go somewhere and talk!"

"Of course we do." She put her hand on his arm, and they went out of the assembly hall; he was glad he had worn his Glen-plaid suit—with the flatted seams.

It was a bit early for dinner. They went into the hotel bar and ordered cocktails and talked, their heads close across the small table, their eyes searching the other's face.

After an hour they moved to the dining room and ordered. People were about them—a birthday party for a dowager in lavender crepe, her adoring family around her; a table where four men talked business, carloadings and over-the-road costs. . . .

But Libby and Dewey talked to each other and noticed no one else. There was so much to say—the years had been many. Her past years and his—what they had done. No, Libby had never married.

"All the good men went away to war, Dewey."

"A lot came back."

"Not you."

"Why . . . Oh, well, no, I didn't come back to the hospital. If that's what you mean."

Her eyes said that it was what she had meant.

They came up to the present. Dewey had already made a speech about what he was doing now.

Libby lifted her coffee cup. "Small hospital—a boat—a

fat cocker spaniel—and a wife?"

"That's the picture."

"When did your hair turn white?"

"It was beginning while I was still an intern. By the time I was thirty, I'd made it."

"It's becoming, Dewey."

"I'm sure."

She laughed. "You always were an idiot. You don't have children?"

"I'm sorry—no."

She nodded.

"Now, tell me about you, Libby."

"Oh—well, I live here in town. I'm one of a dozen—two dozen—anesthetists at the Lincoln Group. When I saw that you would be on the panel today, I came to see what you looked like. I hoped you would be fat and— What's wrong?"

He was leaning toward her, his blue eyes staring.

"It's Kismet!" he answered, his tone awed.

She smiled uncertainly. "Do you know what you are saying?" she asked. "Or did that second martini just catch up with you?"

He laughed. "I'm making sense," he assured her. "Let me tell you."

He ate the last bit of his steak and looked around for the waiter. "I always have peppermint ice cream here," he told Libby, "with fudge sauce."

She laughed. "How do you keep your girlish figure?"

"Easy. Hazel doesn't let me have such things at home."

"Tell me about Hazel."

"No, I want to tell you about Kismet."

He ordered their desserts and more coffee. "Listen," he said, leaning forward. "When I left the hospital at home this noon—it seems much longer ago than that!—I was told to bring an anesthesiologist back with me. And what do I find in the audience? What do I find eating dinner just across the table from me—"

"You invited me."

"I did. Strictly non-partisan. But when I last saw you, Libby, you were going to be a female surgeon."

"That was before I tried to be any kind of a surgeon."

"Sure. So it was Fate which decided you to be an anesthesiologist."

"I'm not very good."

"You have to be good, to work at Lincoln."

"But I'm not Staff. I'm not a teacher."

"Well, that's good."

She stared at him. "What's good about it?"

"Because you will listen more readily to my persuasion to come up the road with me and work at Bayard."

"Oh, Dewey, don't be crazy!"

"Who's crazy? We need an anesthesiologist. You are an anesthesiologist. And I have means of persuading you . . ."

"What means would those be?"

She was smiling now, and her eyes were shining.

"Oh, there's my winsome ways—the pleasure of my company, a six-dollar steak, not to mention those ninety-five cent drinks which I could do better at home for seventeen cents flat."

She laughed merrily, and heads turned to look their way.

"But you didn't know I was an anesthesiologist when you began your blandishments," she reminded Dewey.

"No. There old man Kismet helped me. He often looks after me, you know. When I make a snap diagnosis, when I decide to use a seven iron out of a bad lie, when I come down here hunting an anesthesiologist and find you . . . Seriously, Libby, we do need you. And you'd love it in Bayard. You'd like the staff men. Hazel would take you under her wing—"

"Oh, now, look, Dewey!"

"But she would! She's a swell girl!"

"And any wife loves to meet up with her husband's old girl friend," drawled Dr. Gillis. "Of *course* she does!"

"Oh, Hazel knows she has me hobbled. You'd like living

19

in Bayard—the river—you'd have time of your own. I'll bet your hours at Lincoln are murder."

They were murder.

Libby ate some of her lime sherbet. Then she glanced up at Dewey who was watching her.

"Do you have the authority to ask me?"

"Not to hire you in a firm contract. No. We men do things in joint project. But honest Injun, Libby, they did tell me to bring one of you home. And we do need you. The work would be interesting and the pay good. I could promise that. At least—the very least you could do for an old friend would be to come up and see the place."

She nodded. That was the least she could do. She glanced at her watch.

"I go on call at nine," she explained. "All right, Dewey. I'll come up to Bayard. If the other men want me to. Are they all as attractive as you are?"

He flushed. "Well, of course not. But you can't have everything, Dr. Gillis!"

She picked up her coffee cup. "I'll try to content myself with having you around again," she said lightly.

It was later, much later—in cold truth, it was very late indeed—when Dewey Windsor started home that night. Hazel would have his ears.

And the first thing she would ask would be, "Did you have a good time?" So friendly, so interested. . . .

He hunched his shoulders.

He had had a good time. He certainly had. Once the business of getting an anesthesiologist was out of the way, he and Libby had talked and talked. All about the old gang— where they were, what they were doing, what they had done way back when.

Before nine o'clock they had moved to her apartment— and now Dewey guessed it was a damn good thing she'd got a call around eleven-thirty.

Otherwise he might not, even yet, be driving homeward,

the sickle moon low on the horizon, excitement bubbling and fizzing in his blood. He hadn't felt this way in fifteen years—or maybe it was twenty. Young, and strong, and able to do anything he wanted to do! And anxious to see again the girl who had made him feel this way.

Halfway home, out of habit—certainly he was not sleepy! —he stopped for a cup of coffee. Hazel always asked him if he had done this, ignoring the fact that fifty miles wasn't too much of a drive. But Hazel took good care of him—and he had better tone down before he got home to her, too! He must be able to tell her, and the men at the hospital as well— and calmly!—that, yes, he had found an anesthesiologist. A possible one. He'd known the doctor since his intern days; she was going to come up and talk with the staff. . . .

He hoped it would work out.

Yes. Honestly, he did hope it would work out.

Chapter 2

HAZEL WAS MORE CONCERNED ABOUT HIS LOSS OF sleep than interested in the anesthesiologist he had found for the hospital. She urged Dewey to get right to bed and stop talking. She gathered that his speech had gone well. . . .

He wasn't quite sure that she knew, then, that the anesthesiologist was a woman. It really didn't matter. . . .

However, it mattered to the men.

Because, when he was telling about her, Dewey's obvious enthusiasm raised an eyebrow or two.

"Is she good at her job?" Alison Cornel broke in to ask.

"Now, do you suppose Lincoln keeps any kind of personnel that isn't good at the job?" Dewey spoke impatiently.

"They might," said Dr. Shelton thoughtfully. "With the shortages there are."

"Not personnel who give anesthetics, Garde," Bob Ruble protested.

"Of course not!" Dewey agreed with him. "Libby will be good. Don't worry about that."

"Libby, eh?" said Cornel, and the eyebrows went up again.

"I knew her when she was in med school," said Dewey grumpily. He had seen the eyebrows.

"Goodness, is she as old as you are?"

"No. And besides that, she is better preserved."

"You haven't known any med students since you've been in Bayard," Dr. Ruble said thoughtfully.

"Her age," said Dewey stiffly, "only guarantees experience."

"Stability too."

"I'd think so. If she's been at Lincoln for ten years, she's stable on the job. And that's all really that concerns you birds."

"Has she been there that long?"

"Yes." Dewey rose from the table.

"Don't go away mad," Bob told him. "We'd ask the same questions about a man, Windsor."

Yes, they would. And about a man Dewey would not resent their questions.

"You told me to find an anesthesiologist."

"We did," Alison Cornel agreed. "And we are glad you have found one. We'll be glad to meet with her and even happier if we are able to sign her on. So smooth your feathers, son."

"I'm sorry." Dewey looked sheepish. "It's just—well, I have always liked Libby Gillis. And I thought finding her was great luck."

"It probably was, too. Did you fix a date for her to come up here?"

"She said that she would set a definite one; she thought in about two weeks."

"Good. Then we'll talk to her."

Dewey lifted his hand and went out of the dining room.

"I'll bet she's good-looking," said Dr. Shelton thoughtfully.

"And I'll bet Dewey knew her pretty well," said Bob.

"And *I* bet," said the Chief of Staff, "that we'd do better to wait and see this woman before we make any florid decisions about her—or Windsor."

The first of June and Libby Gillis arrived in Bayard on the same sunny morning. A brisk little wind was ruffling the river into whitecaps, and Hazel flew around the house, getting things ready for the visitor. Dr. Gillis was going to stay overnight, and Hazel was giving a dinner party for her that evening. She would spend the day at the hospital, looking the place over and talking to the staff men. In the late afternoon Dewey would bring her home with him.

"What if they decide they don't want her?" asked Ginny Ruble, who had come over to help Hazel.

"Oh, you know men. They would be polite to her, and then, after she goes home, they would write her a letter regretting that, et cetera, et cetera."

"What if she doesn't like them?"

"I suppose she'd follow the same procedure. I've been told that women doctors have to learn to think and do like men."

"Who told you that?"

Hazel shrugged and got down on her knees to wipe the floor under the couch.

Ginny was tidying the plants that stood about the room. She pinched brown leaves from the huge pot of ivy and asked Hazel if she should snip the dead blooms from the African violets.

"Don't touch them!" cried Hazel in alarm. "Look, suppose you get out the plates and things."

Ginny moved obediently toward the dining room. "Are you using the Meissen?" she asked.

"Of course," said Hazel.

"I hope she appreciates it."

Hazel said nothing.

"Nine plates?" Ginny called to her. "Don't dust the *back*s of the pictures, Hazel!"

Hazel flushed and rubbed her forearm across her face. "I'm in a stew," she admitted.

Dewey's wife was a tall woman, and she would have been prettier if she were not so tense about everything.

"Here comes Nan," Ginny told her. "And Gene. They have buckets of roses."

"Yell at them to keep them in the garage," cried Hazel, running that way herself. "I'll fix the bowls—and things— out there."

Ginny shrugged and went on taking china out of the breakfront and carrying the dishes to the counter in the kitchen. Across the breezeway, she could hear the other three wives discussing the flowers, the party, how jittery Hazel was.

"I think it's enough to keep this dame overnight," said Gene Cornel decisively, "without feeling that you have to give a party for her, too."

"Oh, I have to give one," said Hazel solemnly. "The roses are beautiful, Nan."

"Gene brought the yellow ones. She thought they could go into the guest room."

"They will be lovely. I have a copper bowl—"

"Why do you have to give a party?" asked Gene, starting toward the kitchen, bringing a fine perfume of roses with her. "Hi, Ginny."

"Hi. Where did you find that skirt?"

In surprise, Gene looked down at her full green and white skirt. It was clean, but little else could be said for it.

"Oh, it's one Susan doesn't wear any more."

"You'd better not wear her castoffs either," said Ginny Ruble frankly.

Gene shrugged and started for the dining room.

24

"If your shoes are dusty, take them off," said Ginny. "Hazel has cleaned every *inch*!"

Gene sat down in a rush-bottomed chair. "That's what I mean. She's silly to give a party."

"I have to give one," said Hazel. "Ginny, bring me the soup tureen, and I'll put pink and white roses into it for the table."

Ginny fetched the tureen, and Hazel spread newspapers on the table in the breezeway. Nan Shelton brought the flowers and the clippers.

"Why do you *have* to give a party?" Gene persisted.

"Moral support," said Hazel, biting off the stem of a rose. "I need it."

"Why don't you take the dame to the club?"

"Oh, Dewey wants her to see how we live—you know, home cooking, our friends . . . He's trying to sell Bayard to her."

"If you get any more nervous . . ."

"I won't. You know I always go into a tizzy about a party. Then, when everything is ready, I calm down."

"Yeah, to a mild frenzy. What are you serving?"

Hazel told them. Cornish hens, wild rice, asparagus, a light salad, cheese bread, strawberries and ice cream. "I baked the cookies yesterday."

"I'll wash the asparagus," Nan offered.

"I haven't dug it yet."

"Hazel!" The chorus came in exactly on cue.

"Well, I haven't. I wanted it perfectly fresh."

"Give her canned. Or frozen. A city woman won't know the difference."

"Maybe not," said Hazel hardly, "but Dewey especially asked me to be nice to *this* city woman, and—"

"Why?" asked Gene Cornel bluntly. She brushed her red hair back from her face.

Hazel flushed, and her blue eyes were distressed. "Oh," she said, "he wants her to take the job at the hospital. He wants her to, very much. You know, he's had to do most of their anesthesiology—it's meant longer hours for him, and quite a lot of study—"

"That's true," Gene agreed.

"I'll go cut your asparagus," said little Ginny Ruble. "We'll all help you, Hazel. We'll get everything ready by noon, then you can just *flop* this afternoon, and—"

"If I have time," Hazel was saying, "I'm going down to Leach's and try on that aqua chiffon."

Ginny almost dropped a cup. Nan made a gulping sound. Gene just stared at Hazel.

"For heaven's sake!" she cried. "I was going to wear my hopsacking."

"You can," said Hazel. "But you don't need the moral support I'll need this evening."

"We're doctors' wives, too," said Nan Shelton. "If Dewey wants us to help sell Bayard to this woman—"

"Dewey knew her when she was in school," said Hazel solemnly. "And that's the way he still sees her. Me—he's seen me every day for all the years we've been married, and unless tonight I look really special—and do special things— he isn't going to see me at all."

Her friends comforted her; her friends laughed at her gently, but at noon, when they returned to their homes, they were still concerned about Hazel. She was trying too hard, Gene told Nan.

"How hard is that?" asked Nan solemnly. She was the youngest of the doctors' wives.

At the hospital, Libby Gillis came breezing in about ten o'clock, sleeveless beige linen dress, brown leather belt, matching brown bag and pumps—her hair smartly cut and shining dark, her face vivid . . .

Within minutes, everyone in the building was aware of her. The nurses at the station—Dr. Cornel at the scrub sink —the people in the waiting room—Dr. Windsor, coming briskly across from his office, glad to welcome her!

26

"Wow-eee!" said a patient being taken to x-ray.

Libby laughed, and Dewey grinned, very pleased at the impact she was making.

He talked fast—they'd all gather for lunch, he said. Meanwhile he would take her over to the clinic; there she would eventually meet the chief of staff, Alison Cornel, who had patients waiting. And at lunch . . .

Libby swung into step beside him, and as they went down the corridor, the nurses at the station, the girl at the desk, the patient in the wheel chair, watched them go.

"They make a lovely couple," drawled the older nurse.

Nobody else said a thing.

His office hours attended to, Dewey took Libby on a tour of the hospital, and, as he had promised, the four doctors gathered in the staff dining room for lunch and to meet Dr. Gillis.

They did meet her; they were pleased by her appearance and her manner. They talked and ate—the meal was good. That day, said someone.

"Oh, we feed pretty well as a regular thing," Bob Ruble insisted. "Except on wet hash days—"

"And leftovers from the smooth diets," growled Garde Shelton.

It was typical hospital refectory talk—about the food, the morning's work, polite inquiries as to Dr. Gillis's opinion of their plant.

"When we finish here," said Bob Ruble, "I'll drive you around town. I'll show you the river and both cemeteries . . ."

"Oh, I'm going to do that," said Dewey hastily.

"But—"

"So I have patients!" said Dewey, laughing a little loudly. "Look, Bob—*I* brought Libby here. *I* have a vested interest in the person who may—I hope, I hope!—replace me as utility anesthesiologist. *I* want to show her the town! So—lay off, will you?"

27

Bob sat back with a puzzled frown on his handsome face.

"Don't quarrel about it, boys," Libby said gaily. "I'd really rather none of you would interfere with your routines on my account. Let me wander around on my own, perhaps. I think I could find the river, and I really don't care a lot about the cemeteries."

The little flare-up could have been passed because, just as the men were standing, and ready to go off to their separate offices, an emergency came in which would prevent anyone's escorting Libby anywhere.

She went along to the emergency room, picked a coat off a hook, and when surgery was decided upon, she offered to help.

Dr. Cornel thought it an excellent idea. "That way you and I can see how well we work together!"

Dewey wanted to go in, too, but without Cornel's saying he would be needed . . .

So he went across to his office, feeling, he decided, as anxious as a father would feel with his own son up for orals.

How would Libby do? A stranger in a strange o.r. . . . They were well equipped, but the apparatus would be new to her . . .

And Cornel? He was quite capable of thrusting panic papers at the girl. . . .

About three-thirty Libby returned to Dewey's office; she was smiling serenely. She had had a good session with Dr. Cornel, she said. "He's an excellent surgeon, isn't he?"

"The best," said Dewey. "I'm glad you two hit it off."

"We did. And I am glad, too."

Dewey glanced at his appointment list. "I have one more patient," he said. "Then I'll make quick rounds, and we'll go home. Do you want to wait here?"

"I'll do just that. You can show me your cemeteries on the drive home."

Dewey showed her the river—and they passed one of the cemeteries. He had put her overnight bag into his car; they would leave hers in the hospital lot.

They drove the very long way home. He showed her Cornel's house above the river, the yacht club, the street of fine, tall homes where Dr. Shelton lived. He showed her Fishtown, and the fire station . . .

And finally they came into his garage, laughing.

"We'll get us a cold drink," Dewey promised, for the evening was warm.

Hazel came to greet them; she had not bought the aqua chiffon. She was wearing a white linen dress, very smart and becoming, but not new.

Libby was warmly happy to meet her and took in every feature at a glance. Hazel's beautiful gray hair, her fresh skin, the way her dress fitted her tall, slender body, the white pumps, the blue donkey beads around her throat.

"The first thing," Libby cried, "I want to see your flowers. Dewey has told me so *much* about them!"

"I'm afraid," said Hazel uneasily, "with so much to do, I wouldn't have time—and you'll want to dress. We're having the doctors and their wives for dinner, you know. Did you take her bag in, Dewey?"

"Not yet," he said. He took Libby's arm and led her through to the patio and to Hazel's flower garden. "You have to see the sweet peas," he told Dr. Gillis. "Not to mention the bleeding hearts."

They looked at the flowers, they laughed, they stood talking, and finally they sat down in chairs on the patio, still talking. "I'd get you that drink," said Dewey, "but with a party on, I'm not a brave enough man to go into the kitchen."

Hazel watched them from the window, and she became increasingly nervous. Both Dr. Gillis and Dewey should be dressing—and Dewey, at least, soon enough that Hazel could pick up the wet towels he always left around. It was six o'clock! And . . .

She came out to the patio with this reminder, her tone a little sharp.

"Isn't Lena here to help?" Dewey asked her.

"Yes, she is. But—"

Dewey laughed. "You have to help *her!*" he said, glancing in amusement at Libby.

Inside the house the telephone rang, and Hazel groaned. She had known something like this would happen!

It had. Lena's face appeared at the window. "It's for de doctah!" she cried lustily.

Dewey came back to say that he would have to go downtown—a man was sick at the bus station.

"Make it quick!" Hazel urged him.

"And don't carry off my suitcase!" said Libby.

"I won't. Come with me and get it. And then you'd better dress, my girl. Time's a-wastin'."

"It certainly is," muttered Hazel, watching them. They were so *gay!*

"I can dress in twenty minutes, my man!" Libby was saying.

"Then you're the world's marvel," Dewey assured her.

She was evidently just that, because she did dress in twenty minutes, shower and all. And she came out of the guest room looking lovely and cool in something shimmering and clinging and pale green just as Dewey returned to ask Hazel what she was "all het up about?"

He ducked into the bedroom before she could think of an answer.

The guests arrived. Dewey came out in time to serve the drinks. Hazel told Lena to straighten the bathroom.

The dinner table was beautiful, and the dinner was good. Nine, of course, was an awkward number. "I should have invited someone for Dr. Gillis," Hazel told Ginny Ruble.

"She's getting along just fine with the four men she has," said Ginny coolly.

"Yes, she is, isn't she? She's good-looking, Ginny."

"She's stunning."

"Is Rosalind Russell going to take the job?" asked Gene

Cornel, joining them.

The others laughed and moved on.

Libby didn't notice any awkwardness in the table seating. She talked to the men beside her, to Bob Ruble across from her, and to Garde Shelton at the far end of the table. They all talked together. The men even talked shop—medicine—to this woman. They let her talk it to them. As they never allowed their wives . . .

Dewey told about his call to the bus station. The "sick" man was drunk. He was amusing in the telling. And then the five doctors talked about the laws for alcohol detection, first getting technical and then hilarious. They cited experiences —Libby could tell of her difficulties with accident cases who had alcohol in their blood . . .

"And those who want a nip for the road," she added.

She was beautiful; she was intelligent—clever; her voice was deep; her smile was ready and vivid. She lifted her handsome head above a long and handsome throat; she gestured restrainedly with beautiful hands. The men all enjoyed her.

And their wives watched her, their faces odd.

"I might as well have served hot dogs and sauerkraut," mourned Hazel when the meal was over.

"Oh, she enjoyed her food!" said Nan.

"I didn't," said Hazel glumly.

"Look," said Gene Cornel, "why don't you let me take this woman home with me for the night?"

"Why should you?"

"Well, she and Alison would work together—if she stays here. While Dewey—"

"Dewey is acting like a sixteen-year-old boy who's just discovered women!" said Hazel tartly.

Gene grinned in a sickly way.

"Anyway," Hazel asked her, "what makes you think you're safe?"

"I don't," Gene conceded. "I don't think any of us is."

"I don't know whether to study medicine or grow six

inches," said exquisite, and tiny, Ginny Ruble.

"Oh, Ginny," said Nan reproachfully.

"Make no mistake about it," Ginny told her. "This is a dame!"

The wives clustered at one end of the patio, the men—and Libby—at the other.

"They would say they were interviewing her," drawled Gene.

"Mhmmmnn. All about the best place in St. Louis to get *Sauerbraten*."

"Why do you suppose she hasn't married?" asked Nan Shelton. "She good-looking, witty—clever—"

"Why should she have narrowed things down to one man?" Hazel asked. Then she bit her lip. "I only hope she doesn't start doing that now."

Her friends protested, but they felt that Hazel had some cause to be apprehensive. Dewey was acting as if he had just produced this woman in a lab test tube. He was proprietary; he was appreciative. He beamed at each word she said. He stood, or sat, close to her.

"And she must be a very good doctor!" Nan offered.

"Do you think they will take her in?" asked Ginny. "The hospital, I mean."

Gene Cornel flapped her hand in the direction of the lively group eight feet away. "Unless we object . . ."

"Well, we can't do that!" cried Ginny.

"No," Gene agreed. "We certainly cannot."

Chapter 3

LIBBY GILLIS, HAZEL TOLD, HAD LEFT THE fragrance of her perfume in the Windsor guest room. "Though she was as neat as a pin," she told her friends.

"Not even a dust of powder on the glass of the dressing table. But—I know she was here."

The hospital knew that she'd been there, too. At first the men did not say much about her. A day went by, a second day. Dewey continued to serve as anesthetist when he was needed, but finally there came a late afternoon when the four men gathered in the doctors' room for a half hour of talk, to relax from the tensions of their day, to change from hospital clothes and from hospital thinking before they went home to their families.

"It will take some planning around here if Dr. Gillis does come into our staff," mused Dr. Cornel.

The other men glanced at him and nodded. Her coming would—might—threaten the closeness of these four, and there was unspoken regret.

"She'd not be an owner . . ." said Bob Ruble finally.

"And we couldn't ask her to share this room what with the showers and all," said Garde firmly.

"The day she helped Cornel, she changed in the nurses' room."

"That's what she would have to do, of course," Dewey agreed.

"She worked well . . ." said the Chief of Staff. "Efficient. Quiet."

"Mhmmmnnn. She asked very intelligent questions when I talked to her," said Bob.

"I liked her manner. An anesthetist has a special problem with children," said Dr. Shelton.

"Libby was a good solid student," Dewey contributed. All of the men were wary about showing too much enthusiasm. Dewey had toned his down. That was why three days had elapsed before this discussion. The men had not wanted to appear to jump; Dewey had not wanted to seem to push. They must, of course, consider this important move calmly and seriously.

"What makes you the most nervous?" Bob Ruble asked

Dewey. "The thought that she'll move in here or that she won't?"

Dewey's cheeks reddened. "Why should I be nervous at all?" he demanded. Another word, and he would flare like tinder.

"Well, I thought that this past romance of yours might be an item."

Dewey picked up a sample package of gloves and slit the cellophane with his thumbnail.

"It was just one of several," he said quietly.

"Several *romances?*" Bob cried. "Why, Dewey—"

Dewey's eyes lifted. "I've been married to Hazel for a *long* time." There was warning in his tone.

"That's not the point," said Alison Cornel thoughtfully.

"I certainly hope it won't be," Dewey agreed. He thrust his hand into one of the gloves and waggled his fingers, looking at them.

His friends ventured to look at each other.

"We need a doctor of this sort," said Dewey carefully, taking off the gloves.

"We do," said Dr. Cornel. "And we probably couldn't find a more suitable one willing to come here to work."

Garde Shelton opened his mouth to say something, then closed it again. His cheeks were red.

"Her record is good," continued Cornel, after the short pause. "I've talked to a few men at Lincoln—"

Dewey's head lifted, then he shrugged and nodded. Of course the chief of staff had to do things of that sort.

"We all talked to Dr. Gillis," Dr. Cornel continued. "I have heard no strong expressions of dislike or disapproval." He looked around the room. No man spoke in disagreement. "So . . ." He stood up. "Should we try it?"

Again he looked around the room, and each man's head nodded, each face spoke agreement.

"Fine," said Dr. Cornel. "I think we should, too. I wonder—" He looked at his watch; he looked at Dewey. "Would she be at the hospital?"

Dewey shrugged. "I'd try there first," he advised.

The call went through. Dr. Gillis was at her home. The number was given, Dr. Cornel called it, and she answered. In the doctors' room at Bayard there was a sigh of relief. Now, they felt, one more hour of suspense would have been unendurable.

They listened intently to Alison's brief conversation. He didn't really need to tell what had been said, but he did anyway. "She'll come," he said as he set the phone down. "First of the week—ready to go to work. She's already given the hospital notice. That suit you, Windsor?"

Dewey looked up in surprise. "Sure it suits me. What do you think I've been working for? I—"

The men were laughing at him, and he nodded, shamefaced. "All right, all right," he agreed. "Have your fun."

Dr. Cornel began to change his clothes. "I hope this thing will work out, and smoothly," he said earnestly. "Because we already have troubles enough in our little group."

Each man stopped what he was doing to look at him questioningly. Trouble? Other than their slight uneasiness over Dewey's handling of the Gillis situation—what trouble?

"Gene," said Gene's husband, "is upset about her brother these days. And when Gene is upset—about anything—it is bound to affect me. That means the rest of you will feel the shock wave." No one smiled. The three men were staring at him in astonishment.

"I didn't know Gene *had* a brother!" said Bob Ruble bluntly.

"Or any family . . ." said Dewey, more softly.

"Well, of course she has a family!" cried Dr. Cornel. "What did you birds think? That she was some sort of mushroom?"

Dewey laughed. "If so," he conceded, "she makes a pretty good mushroom. Though, really, Cornel—"

Alison turned to his locker. "I know," he admitted. "But —as a matter of fact, she has a rather large family."

Now the men looked at one another. "But why haven't we known?" cried Bob Ruble. "She never speaks of a family."

"I've never heard them mentioned," Garde Shelton agreed.

"Certainly haven't seen any of 'em," Dewey contributed.

But each man was thinking, and Alison, when he turned, could read their thoughts. They had always known that Gene was a person of reserves. Pleasant, friendly, even blunt about her daily interests, they had suspected, each one of them, and for various reasons, a resentment in Gene of her past which made her silent about that past.

"She—" Alison was saying. "She has small contact with her family."

His face was very pink, and his eyes looked troubled.

"You see, they are not the sort of family we are accustomed to around here."

Dewey sat down in one of the chairs, looking as if he would make no move to go home until this point was cleared up. "What in thunder do you mean by that?" he demanded. *"Sort of families!"*

Dr. Cornel took a deep breath and walked over to the mirror to arrange his tie and collar. "There are people," he said evasively, "who live differently, you know." He picked up his coat and put it on. "They have other interests . . ." He strode to the door, opened it, and went through, closing it behind him.

The men left in the doctors' room looked at that door and then they looked at each other. "I see what he means about upsetting us all," murmured Garde Shelton.

"But what did he *mean*?" insisted Dewey. *"Not the sort of family—people who live differently . . ."* He scrubbed his fist through his hair. "I don't get it!"

"It is evidently a painful subject," said Bob.

"So it's painful. Then why mention it at all? They haven't, you know, for the years we've known Gene and Alison. She's always been that mushroom he spoke of."

"Calm down, Windsor," Dr. Ruble advised. "We are close friends, but there is always a line drawn—"

"I concede the line, Bob. But since Cornel brought up the subject . . ."

"Yes, you're right. He lifted the wire and invited us to crawl under."

"At least to notice that there is a wire," mused Grade. "Families—there could have been a fight of some sort. Families have them."

"Uh-huh. Over wills and things."

"Or a disgrace of some sort."

"Maybe they disapproved of Gene's marriage."

"How could they?"

Bob shrugged. "Eye of the beholder," he reminded his friends.

"I've always known," said Dewey "and the rest of you birds have, too, that there was *something*—"

"Yes," Bob agreed. "It shows in her attitude to both of her daughters. She analyzes them, especially Carol."

"She used to talk about that girl's feeling of rejection. Carol has been made to know that she isn't as outgoing, or as pretty, as Susan," Garde said. "I've tried to talk to Gene about it."

"Get anywhere?"

"Maybe. A little way. Carol seems to be turning into a lovely young woman. I told Gene the idea of rejection in babyhood was ridiculous."

"It can happen."

"It can. But not with a mother who literally breathes for her daughters. In fact, I think Gene is too possessive."

"Well, if her own past history is—I wonder what in hell did happen."

Bob went to his locker and changed his coat. "I'm going

home. This discussion is a silly project. The Cornels will tell us what they want us to know. Even if this is a difficult time for them, and if it affects us, we are going to have to wait and take each thing as it comes. We have never pried into each other's affairs, and I don't think we should start now."

"No prying, eh?" said Dewey. "I can't buy a new pair of shoestrings without at least three boards of inquiry and estimate set up."

"Shoestrings, yes," said Garde Shelton, smiling. "But we haven't really probed into your past with Dr. Gillis, have we?"

"You've tried," said Dewey darkly. "You've tried. Only my long-established habit of taciturnity—"

Garde threw a towel at his head, and Dewey laughed.

The men finished dressing and went out into the hospital corridor. "I still think we should wait and see," Dr. Shelton advised.

"About Gene and her family?"

"Yes. That is what I meant. But maybe we should apply it to Dewey and Dr. Gillis, too. Let's just see what comes and how."

"All you'll get on the Windsor ledger," Dewey informed him, "will be a record of more of my patients attended to once I don't have to put on greens and sit on that damn stool in o.r."

"That's what Garde meant," said Bob. "We'll wait and see."

Laughing, the three men went their separate ways.

Chapter 4

BY THE SECOND WEEK IN JUNE SUMMER HAD definitely come to the river town of Bayard. The trees that dipped their branches into the water's edge were full-leaved; the shadows cast by them were richly brown. Offshore, the great basin of the river gleamed with diamond dust, and the river patrol put-putted lazily among such boats as were out on a weekday morning.

Far toward the Illinois shore a line of barges inched upstream, laundry hanging from a line on one of them. An outboard threw a silver spray, and the patrol stopped to exchange greetings with the fishing party on the pontoon craft thirty feet from shore.

"That looks like fun," said Nan Shelton, watching her small daughter lest she stagger too far away through the beach's sand.

"A pontoon?" asked Gene. "You're too young for that sort of thing, Nan."

"I'm not too young for anything that looks peaceful," said Nan firmly. "With two lively young ones under foot, and relatives coming for the weekend . . ."

"Your relatives, or Garde's?"

"Garde's mother."

No one said anything, tactfully. Garde's mother was a sweet woman, a schoolteacher, who would, if allowed, smother her family with affection and firm direction. Nan and Garde were always lovely to her; Nan, at least, was always exhausted after a weekend with the elder Mrs. Shelton in the house.

"Last time . . ." mused Ginny Ruble.

Nan smiled. Last time Mrs. Shelton had insisted that Nan put underwear—T shirt and panties—on the children under their pajamas. It would, she had said, give them a sense of security.

"She raised her boys by working very hard," Nan reminded her friends. "Fiddle!" her voice lifted. "Come back!"

Fiddle turned around, smiled enchantingly, and sat down hard on the sand, her black curls bouncing.

"She wants us to start young Garde in piano," Nan said in a small voice. "She thinks he has talent."

"Butch is too young," said Gene emphatically. No one but Nan ever called the little boy anything but Butch.

"Yes," Nan agreed. "But we have to listen to his grandmother and be tactful."

"Families are just pure hell!" said Gene explosively, lying back on the sand and dropping her head scarf across her face.

The other women looked her way expectantly.

"Have I told you," Gene asked, "that my brother is coming to visit us? Not for a long visit—just a few days."

She had not told them—that, or anything, about this brother.

"Why," asked Ginny Ruble, speaking carefully, "haven't you ever told us about your brother, Gene?"

The three husbands had each in his own way told the women about Alison's revelations, each adding the word that nothing should be said unless Gene herself mentioned the matter. Alison had reported that she was upset about some present crisis—or situation.

"Just be friendly and wait," Bob had said to Ginny.

"Don't let on that we've been talking," said Dewey to Hazel.

"I think the best way is to be receptive," Garde told Nan. "No more."

But now—Gene had mentioned the brother. He was coming to Bayard for a short visit.

"I haven't talked about my family at all," Gene was saying now, her voice muffled, perhaps by the handkerchief over her face. "The—er—the relationship has been—I suppose you might call it strained."

No one commented. Nan got up and went down the beach after Fiddle, brought her back to the group, shook her red sand bucket invitingly at the child. Ten feet behind them, Butch was happily riding a driftwood log.

"My mother . . ." said Gene, after a long pause. "Well—sometime, maybe, I'll tell you about my mother."

Hazel, Ginny, Nan—each was formulating a mental picture of Gene's mother. A tall, clubwoman type—a soft, smothering type—a whining hypochondriac—what sort of mother would Gene have? Herself wiry, redheaded, brusquely impatient with life's perversities which, as often as not, she blamed on her children, her husband, and her friends.

She was loyal, blunt, and a sentimentalist, though she would have roughly denied the charge.

But—what sort of mother had produced lovable and loving Gene?

"I had to speak of my family now," she said gruffly, "because Shawn is coming, and you'll know about it. Maybe you'll meet him."

Maybe? The four families had always shared their experiences, good or bad, interesting or dull. This weekend someone would arrange a gathering somewhere because Garde's mother would be a guest. It wasn't necessary, except to the closeness that was an integral part of this group. So when Gene's brother came . . .

"Is he a—younger brother, Gene?" Ginny asked diffidently.

Gene bounced a little on the sand. "Oh, yes," she said gruffly. "Of course. Lots younger. In fact, he's still in school. That is, he's just finishing his first-year study for the priesthood. In the Episcopal Church."

The three women who were her audience all sat up, stiffly erect. "Wha-at?" said Nan's soft lips soundlessly. Gene herself had gone into the Episcopal Church only this year. . . .

Now to have her tell . . . Again their imaginations splintered like the light upon the river's waters.

It was too much for them to comprehend—everything in a rush this way—a brother for Gene—and training—to be . . . The church had never seemed to mean very much to

Gene. Individually the others in the group had decided that she had grown up in an atmosphere which did not include the church as an essential part of life. It had been Alison who decided that his family would put themselves in the way of attending church and taking a part in its life, allowing it to take a part in theirs.

But—not even to Nan Shelton, whose father had been a clergyman—had Gene ever hinted . . .

"Please tell us?" said Nan now, her voice trembling.

"Oh, yes." Gene sat up, tied her scarf around her throat, and began to pull at its ends. "I don't know how familiar you are with what it takes to study for the ministry."

"Nan surely knows a lot," said Hazel dryly.

"Yes," Gene agreed. "More than I do."

"Has your whole family been Episcopalians?" Ginny asked. "All along?"

"No." Gene's lips pressed thin. "Shawn was confirmed during his senior year at the university. He—he goes deeply into things. Emotionally, I mean."

"Do you see him a lot, Gene?" asked Hazel.

"No, I don't. But lately—I've heard from him." Evidently it was hard for her to talk about this brother. Her habit of not speaking of her family had become firmly ingrained.

"Last year," she began again, "oh, it was longer than that —but, roughly, last year, he decided to study for the ministry. And—this is true in a lot of churches—Lutheran, Roman Catholic, even men studying to be rabbis—there are certain psychological tests which are given before a man is allowed to enroll. They are given again—or maybe new ones —at the end of the first year. Just their names would send me into a tizzy."

She picked up a small stick and began to trace patterns in the sand between her knees. "Names like Thematic Apperception Test. The Guilford-Zimmerman Temperament Survey . . ."

"Goodness," gasped Ginny. "Did he pass?"

Gene looked at her, and her face was drawn, a little pale under the summer freckles. "These are routine," she said carefully. "Alison lately has looked into the matter, and he knows all about it. These tests are given at the beginning and again after a year's study. But—no—Shawn didn't pass. I mean, he had some difficulty." She looked exactly as when one of her girls failed to make the honor roll at high school.

Sarah Ruble came running up to ask her mother, breathlessly, for money to get a Coke. "I'm thusty!" she declared dramatically.

Ginny produced the coin so quickly that Sarah stood uneasy for a minute, and Ginny waved her on.

"Wasn't he suited for the thing, Gene?" she asked sympathetically, but eagerly, too. "I mean, just everyone isn't suited to be a clergyman."

"I don't know just what the trouble was, or is," said Gene carefully. "Last year Shawn said that studying for the priesthood might balance his emotional stresses. But now—well, maybe he isn't suited. Anyway, he is upset at some things that have happened, and he has asked if he may come here and talk to Alison."

Her friends laughed, each in her own way. Hazel quickly, abruptly; Ginny as if she were honestly amused; Nan as if it hurt a little to laugh, and yet she, too, was struck by the absurdity of the young man's seeking advice from a *surgeon!*

"What can Alison do?" asked Ginny. "I should think a psychiatrist—"

"Oh, Ginny, Shawn has seen psychiatrists. They give the tests, I'm pretty sure. But since he wants to talk to Alison, of course he may. And Alison says he then will probably talk to a psychiatrist. Maybe bring a new man into the picture. But for now, with all we have to go on—that Shawn had difficulty with the tests and is upset—well anyway—he's coming."

"How old is he, Gene?" Hazel asked.

"Ten years younger than I am."

Hazel nodded. "That might do it," she said.

"Do what?" Now all attention turned to Hazel.

She shrugged. "I think maybe you should marry him off to Libby."

Her friends stared at her, then Gene herself laughed. The others joined in. For ten days these wives had been holding back, not discussing the new doctor at the hospital. This morning Hazel had opened the floodgates. Gene's brother was forgotten in the spate of absurd idea and comment, laughter, and surmise.

Did anyone ever see such clothes as Dr. Gillis wore? they asked. She's smart—oh, definitely! And all the time! I have never seen her mussed or ruffled! She's a wow on the club veranda! I hate to think what she manages in the doctors' room.

"That's out of bounds."

"How do you know?"

"Dewey told me."

"You asked him?"

"I don't think so. But—he told me."

"She's living in one of those new apartments on Missouri Avenue."

"They say Willard Laurent has bought new binoculars."

"Gene!"

"Well, she sun-bathes. And when you consider what she does here on the beach—what must she do on her own balcony?"

"I think that is definitely catty."

"I'm sorry."

"You don't sound it."

Gene laughed. "I think Willard would be much better for Dr. Gillis than Shawn. He's been a widower just long enough, and he does seem interested."

"A lot of men—people—seem interested in her. We are."

"She went on a trip with the Copelands this past weekend . . ."

"Last Saturday she danced a storm at the club . . ."

"She plays golf . . ."

"And swims . . ."

"When does she work?"

"Bob says she's good."

"So does Dewey." Now Hazel drew pictures on the sand.

"Does she get along with the hospital personnel?"

"Frankly, I think there has been some trouble. One of the nurses says she is too outspoken."

"And in that voice . . ."

"She's lively—"

"And seems to make her own fun, wherever she is."

"Which is a good many places. Active is the word for our Dr. Gillis."

"One afternoon this past week—" Hazel began, then stopped.

"Tell us!" Gene demanded.

"Maybe Dewey would think I shouldn't mention it."

"We'll deal with Dewey."

"At home? When he comes in, cross as a bear, because someone has been nawsty to Libby Gillis?" Hazel's cheeks were scarlet, her voice sharp.

"Oh, Hazel!" said Ginny mournfully.

Hazel dashed the back of her hand across her eyes. "He won't allow anyone to criticize that woman!" she declared. "What she says—wears—does. If she can't be found when needed at the hospital, he makes excuses. If she gets into a row with the o.r. girls, they're to blame. I'll bet he gave Bill Stevens a proper talking to for writing her a warning ticket!"

"*Bill?*" The others gaped at Hazel. Bill Stevens was the official water patrol. And a warning ticket . . .

"She doesn't have a boat, too, does she?" asked Nan.

"Oh, of course not!" said Hazel. "She took out Dewey's—"

"Without asking him?"

"I think so, but he didn't really say so. He got told about the registration item, of course. All he said was that he'd have to give Libby a course in marine law."

"And won't that be fun and games?" drawled Gene.

"I'd not want to take his boat without asking—"

"Nor me," said Hazel. "But Gillis—that seems to be different."

Her friends were sorry. They hoped Hazel was unduly upset. But . . .

"How is she working out at the hospital?" asked Nan politely. "I mean, her work and all."

"The men sound enthusiastic," said Ginny Ruble.

"About her work?"

Ginny shrugged. "I hope."

Chapter 5

GENE LIKED GETTING UP EARLY, AS EARLY AS ALISON left for the hospital and his surgery schedule, before her family was stirring. Especially in summer she liked to do this— to go out on the front stoop to look up at the trees, trying to locate the oriole that sang so piercingly from a high branch, to note the silver glimmer of dew upon the grass, to look down through the woods, a mystery of green leaves and brown shadows, on down to the river that was faintly hazed with mist and seemed not to move at all. King, the boxer, came to her and nudged her knee affectionately with his great thick head; a squirrel chittered amiably from the oak tree, and a robin decided to join his cousin the oriole in early-morning song.

Gene stepped down to the walk and gingerly into the wet grass, to pick up the morning paper. King bit at it playfully, and she held it out of his reach. Then, smiling, she walked back to the stoop, rolling the paper more tightly so that she could slip it out of the string; this she dropped into the pocket of her housecoat, murmuring to herself to remember to take the string out before she washed the robe.

She shook the paper open and stood for a long minute looking at the picture on the front page. Her eyes moved to the headlines.

She blinked her eyelids and moved so that her head shadowed the page from the sun. Yes, there it was. In black letters.

ADDIE BURKE RETIRES

And there was the picture.

There was also the half-column telling that Addie Burke was a renowned—a world-renowned—a well-loved pianist.

Who was retiring.

An award was to be made—in New York for her achievements professionally.

Gene's hand went out toward the latch of the screen door. She continued to read. Addie Burke—wife—mother—remarkable person . . .

Gene looked at the picture. It was not a new one—the open piano—the smile . . .

Standing in the warm sunshine, with the scent of roses heavy in the air, Gene shivered. She folded the paper carefully and went into the house, her own shadow preceding her across the parquetry floor of the wide center hall. Sunlight poured in through the screen, tracing the shadow of the curved stair rail against the green and silver wallpaper.

Walking carefully, as if doing the thing mechanically from habit, Gene put the paper on the table in the living room—where it was always put—"for Father, whenever he comes home."

She drew back the rosy gauze curtains and looked out of the big window—flagged terrace, sloping lawn, the wooded valley behind the house. . . .

Sighing, she went into the kitchen; she set the table and filled the juice glasses, which she put back into the refrigerator. Someday she would figure out how to put the refrigerator closer to the sink and the work counter. She opened the back door for the cat who had been sleeping with one of the girls—against rules, but generally done.

She washed her hands and got out a carton of eggs, a box of cereal. She poured herself a cup of coffee and thoughtfully put three strips of bacon in the pan. That would bring Susan down. It had better. She was on duty as junior life guard that morning. Carol could drive her, if Carol got up. . . .

Gene went to the stairs and called, "Susan!" loudly, then clapped her hand over her mouth; she'd forgotten their house guest. Having remembered him, she went into the bathroom adjoining her bedroom—and Alison's—and ran a comb through her red hair. She picked up a lipstick and put it down again. No one would believe her if she appeared at breakfast wearing lipstick.

She went back to the kitchen, made two slices of toast, took them and the bacon to the table, and sat down. She must plan today—the meals, where the car would need to be . . .

Susan came in, sleepy, swollen-faced, her pajamas rumpled.

"Go back and wash," said her mother automatically. "Do you want an egg?"

Susan made a face, and Gene nodded. "Go wash," she said again.

The girl went only to Gene's bathroom and came back quickly. "I'm on Guard," she reminded her mother.

"I know. Carol will drive you. I suppose it would be too much to expect you to walk."

"Oh, Mother . . ."

"You're getting chubby in all the wrong places, Susan."

"I've been told. I've been told." Susan drank her orange juice; she poured milk on her cereal. Gene gave her the plate with bacon and two pieces of toast. She took the sugar bowl to the other end of the table. Susan sniffed.

48

King wanted in—the cat came with him. Gene fed them both down in the garage. The teakettle whistled, and the phone rang.

Day was started in the Cornel home—the animals, the people, the sounds. . . .

Carol came downstairs, trim in a robe of dark-blue jersey. She didn't want an egg. Could she have cinnamon toast? No bacon. She'd drink milk but wanted no cereal.

Her hair was brushed. She looked, as usual, neat, a thing her mother envied her older daughter.

While the bread was toasting, Carol went into the living room and brought back the newspaper. Gene was telling Susan exactly what her schedule for the day must be. "I'll be busy. You'll have to see to a few things." She put Carol's toast on a plate, and got the cinnamon-and-sugar "egg" from a shelf in the cabinet.

"Hey, Mom, look!" Carol said, taking the plate, but not lifting her eyes from the paper.

"I saw it," said Gene. "Butter your toast while it's hot." Even as she spoke, she began to butter the toast herself.

Carol reached for the egg and sifted sugar generously on the toast; the fragrance of cinnamon rose richly.

"She must be something!" she cried, putting the folded paper down. "She certainly doesn't look like anybody's grandmother!"

"No . . ." said Gene.

Susan reached across and took the paper out of her sister's hand. "Can she play that good?" she asked.

"She can play that *well*," said Gene, automatically reproving.

Susan nibbled at a piece of bacon. "Do you look like her, Mom?" she asked. "Do we?"

Gene shook her head. Gene did look like Addie. A little. She would not say so. Susan was like Alison—big, strong-featured. Carol had Mike's coloring, but she did look—a little—Gene would not say that, either.

Carol got up for another slice of bread. "Why don't we know her, Mom?" she asked.

Now Gene must say something. "Oh," she managed, as if such things were not important, "she doesn't stand still long enough for anybody to know her."

"I guess not," said Carol, reclaiming the paper, and turning it inside out to read the continuation of the article. "This is a long list of things she's done—places she's played—movies, even. Have you seen any of them?" she looked up at her mother.

"No," said Gene.

"It says here that she maintains a home—"

"What's maintain?" asked Susan.

"For heaven's sake!" cried Gene, glad of a chance to vent some sort of feeling. "Sixteen years old and you don't know *anything!*"

"Yes, I do, Mom. I—"

"Mom maintains a home," Carol instructed. "It just means 'keep house,' knucklehead. In between concerts Addie Burke 'keeps house.' "

"Ha!" said Gene, her voice rasping.

Both girls stopped and looked around at her. "Mom?" asked Carol, her face troubled.

Gene saw the worry in their young eyes. "Oh, don't mind me!" she told them. "I—" She turned on the water and the Disposal noisily.

"Is your Uncle Shawn getting up?" she asked, when the racket stopped.

"His door is shut," Carol reported. "I didn't hear a sound."

"What's the matter with him, Mom?" Susan asked. "Is he sick?"

"I don't know," said Gene readily.

"But he came to see Father—"

"Well, a doctor told Shawn that maybe he shouldn't go on with his studies at the seminary, and he wanted to talk the situation over with Father. It was upsetting to be told he

50

couldn't go on with his plans."

"I like having an uncle," said Susan cozily. "And he's nice—"

"Good-looking," Carol agreed warmly. "A really beautiful man!"

Gene wanted to protest. She could not. Shawn Burke was a really beautiful man—red-blond like Addie, big like Mike, with the charm of both.

"Mary Ruble saw him down at the beach with us yesterday," Carol was saying. "She's drooling. She says what this town has needed is a new man."

Again Gene bit her tongue to keep silent. For years she had not talked about her family. Now, she felt sure, the least said, the better. She was *not* going to let them reach her and hers.

Susan was again reading the paper. "What kind of award will they give her, Mom?" she asked.

"Oh—a platter, or a bowl. Silver, and engraved, of course. There will be a huge bouquet of flowers—speeches—"

"Will we inherit it?"

"Inherit what?"

"The silver bowl or platter."

Gene's lips thinned in exasperation. She should have hidden the newspaper on sight. "I doubt it!" she said sharply.

"Don't you—wouldn't you want it?" Susan and Carol were watching her, wide-eyed.

And Gene gazed at them, feeling helpless. "No-o," she said slowly. "No, I wouldn't want it."

King was barking at the milk truck. Gene started for the door. "You girls had better dress," she said. "Susan has to be at the beach by nine."

When she came in with the milk, the girls had gone upstairs. Gene moved about, clearing the table, setting a fresh place for Shawn. She stacked the dishwasher and sat down on the high stool to make a grocery list. She might be able to manage a trip to the market. If not, Carol would have to shop. She'd sign a check. She sighed and rested her forehead on her hand.

She was worried. About a dozen things. She couldn't talk about those things to the girls. Alison had a vague idea and understanding of her worries, but he was a busy man. She couldn't talk to her friends . . . She wanted to. She even wanted to talk to the girls—to Carol, at least—about her mother. And about Shawn.

She dreaded the day that lay ahead for her—and for him. She was worried for him. He was very sweet—and quiet, some of the time. At other times he was full of life, excited, his eyes bright. He seemed much younger than he was. There was *something* wrong.

But, no, Gene could not talk about it! She had not talked of her family for years, and until lately she had been able to keep from thinking about them; gradually they had melted into the shadows of the years gone by. Now she had her life in Bayard, her home, the girls, her friends—and Alison.

The Burkes—any of them—had no place in this life which she had made here, among her friends, an enviable life in an enviable world made up of hot corn bread, summer apples, aphids on the roses . . .

A world where the biggest excitement could be the advent of a woman like Libby Gillis. Gene rested her chin on her hand, looked out the window at the summer sky, and deliberately thought about Libby. A handsome woman, certainly. Beautiful in everything she did, and she did a lot of things. Yesterday she, too, had been at the beach. Libby was an excellent swimmer. And when she chose to rest, she floated on a long pale-green air mattress, a yellow pillow under her head, and in her perfectly plain one-piece green suit she looked like a sculpture made of gold; her skin, her slender arms, her smooth, long—and slender—legs, gleamed like dull satin. Her face . . . she smiled and drawled answers to those who saw her or called to her. She lay there in the sun, one arm up, her hand under her capped head, the other down at her side, like a picture.

Earlier this summer she had offered excitement enough, and by now the club was literally on its ears over the woman. At the hospital . . .

Alison didn't say a word, other than that she knew her job.

Hazel was worried, and so her friends worried. They must want to worry, because, really, Dewey wouldn't—oh, *no!* Not *ever!*

Later that morning the other three wives gathered on the clubhouse beach. Gene, Susan Cornel had told them, was busy with something she was going to do with her uncle Shawn.

The wives talked a little about Shawn.

He was handsome.

Oh, not really.

Yes, by today's standards he was.

"That puts me in my place!"

"Don't be silly. Styles change in men. Now the big, rugged type is the thing."

"Didn't Gene say that he was only ten years younger than she was?"

"Yes."

"But that would make him—"

"I heard him telling the men that he had not gone to the university straight from prep school, that he'd started, but had walked out, and he then had bummed—he used that *word*—all over the world before he decided that there was some good in a formal education. Then he'd done it in three years."

"And entered the seminary."

"I suppose."

"He doesn't look like a priest to me . . ."

"What does a priest look like?"

The sun was warm; a gentle breeze lifted their hair or the scarves tied over their hair. The children played. Ginny Ruble kept saying she would have to go home, but she continued to sit on the sand, pretty in blue denim and red bandanna. Hazel had brought a small stool. She had swum for a time and now was bundled into a bulky terry robe which she insisted was not hot.

Nan Shelton wore a tan blouse and brown shorts, and she was sketching—a hobby lately taken up. The river and the boats, she said, made fine subjects. "Though the boats keep changing around."

"Dewey says Garde has done some really good paintings," Hazel commented.

"Oh, Garde is good at anything! It is very discouraging." But his wife's tone wasn't entirely cheerful.

The others asked about the visit of her mother-in-law.

"She was all right. She doesn't think the club should serve liquor on Sunday."

"Oh, my."

"Well, she had to find *something*."

"What did she think of Shawn Burke?"

"She didn't mention him. Just said it was nice that the families had all got together while she was here."

Hazel nodded. "I think Gene would have rather—"

"What's wrong there?" It was a question asked many times.

"We'll find out in time."

"I meant with Gene."

"I meant that, too."

There was a little silence, then Ginny, determinedly, began to talk about the plastic pipes which the Kennedys planned to use for their new home.

"Don't they know that those things froze for the Kibblers, and since they couldn't be thawed with heat or anything, that Joann and Little Ike had to haul water from January to March?"

"Maybe they don't know—"

"As if anything ever stayed *unknown* in Bayard!"

"Well," said Nan slowly, "I've about decided that that isn't all bad."

This surprised her friends. She was always trying to discourage gossip.

"No," she continued, "for if we—if the town, our friends at least—had known something about Gene's family, there would not now be so much speculation over the brother who suddenly shows up from nowhere."

"There's speculation all right," said Ginny Ruble. "And Gene really hates it."

"She's certainly unhappy about something. Of course, from the little that has been told us, I suspect she has cause."

"Gene is inclined to go to extremes."

"Yes, she is. But I do feel that it is too bad this thing had to come up this summer."

"But *what* thing, Ginny?"

"I don't know what thing!" Ginny admitted, her pretty eyes troubled. "Just that Gene is all upset about it, and she shouldn't be—not this summer. Now all her thought and interest should be on getting Carol ready to go to college. The first one to go away—I know that can be pretty engrossing."

Ginny's eldest daughter, Mary, would also go to college in the fall, and she, too, was the "first one."

"Do you suppose, if we could pick our times, we'd ever find a good time for troublesome things?" asked Hazel.

"Like headaches, you mean," said Ginny. "No, I don't suppose we would ever be ready. But the truth is Gene will have so much to do—clothes and things. And if Alison is like Bob, he'll insist on Carol's having her teeth checked—her eyes—things like that."

"Gene has talked some about their all taking a trip—this last summer together, she called it."

Her friends smiled fondly. "She's been really upset," Ginny confirmed, "and dubious about letting Carol go away from home at all."

"Carol will do fine," said Nan confidently.

"Yes, I think she will, too," said Ginny. "Garde has helped that girl; she used to be overly emotional and withdrawn."

"It was mostly Gene's fault. Oh, I shouldn't talk about it."

"You don't need to. We all know that Gene has always expected Carol to be difficult. Susan she lets alone."

"Of the two, Susan will be the one to kick up her heels when she goes away to school."

For a minute or two the women looked at Susan, down the beach, perched on the lifeguard's high stool. A handsome girl, a little large, but friendly and impulsive. Her skin was walnut brown; her blond hair was bleached to the color of straw.

"Gene's brother . . ." said Hazel thoughtfully. "He seems to be a charming young man. Really sweet."

"I think," said Ginny, beginning to put things back into her beach bag, "I think he's been sick."

"Oh, he doesn't look—"

"Not that kind of sick! But I think he's either had a nervous breakdown or he is asking for one. I have to go home."

Her friends stared at her. "How do you figure . . . ?"

Ginny got up on her knees and dusted the back of her denim skirt free of sand. "I watched him," she said earnestly. "Yesterday when we had the beach picnic. He'd go off into his own thoughts—his own world. He'd be smiling and holding a hot dog or a Coke, ready to eat, but for a while he just wouldn't be there! Once I saw him looking very, very sad. The next minute he was shouting and roughhousing with the kids. But if you'd watch his hands —nearly all the time they were clenched until his knuckles were white."

"He was intense in everything he said," Hazel confirmed.

"Garde thought he was very smart," said Nan.

"Oh, yes," said Ginny. "He talked on all sorts of subjects and showed that he had read widely. He has traveled—and evidently he is a thinker. But just the same . . ."

Chapter 6

SUSAN SPENT THE MORNING ON THE BEACH AND ate lunch at the club's snack bar. Carol did the marketing with Gene and asked to be dropped off at Cornelia Sims'— they had things to talk about. Yes, she would probably stay for lunch.

This took care of the girls. Susan would get a ride home from the beach when she was ready to come. She'd swim a little and maybe take the dinghy out.

Gene would have, and must have, a mind free of other family affairs. At noon she fixed lunch for herself and Shawn and took their trays out to the porch. They were due at the hospital at one-thirty, she reminded the man who lay on the chaise, his legs stretched out long before him.

Shawn nodded, said thank you for the lunch, and ate moodily in silence. Gene picked up a magazine and read as she ate. She didn't feel like talking either.

At a quarter past one, promptly for her, she backed the car out of the garage and sounded the horn for Shawn, who came out of the front door, asking if he should lock it.

"It will lock itself," said Gene, watching her brother come down the brick walk. He wore a white shirt, dark-blue slacks, a Madras sport coat. The sun gleamed upon his carefully combed hair.

"How far is it?" he asked, settling into the seat and lighting a cigarette.

"About a mile and a half." Gene had on short white gloves. Her dress was blue, the skirt full. She had tied a length of blue net around her hair.

"Is it a big hospital?" Shawn was making polite conversation. His hand had trembled a little when he lit his cigarette.

"Forty beds. Big enough for this town. Yesterday you met

the four doctors."

"Yes. Nice chaps."

They were going to meet with a psychiatrist—the psychiatrist who had, during the past month, examined Shawn, as a consultant on the case. But, since Shawn had been attending a seminary in the East, why was this meeting to take place in Bayard, and with the Alison Cornels?

Gene had to know! So she asked her brother.

The blond young man shrugged. "He asked about my family. He said he wanted to meet them. I told him that you were my family—so—" He shrugged again.

"But *why?*" Gene demanded. "With Addie, and Mike—you shouldn't have, Shawn!"

"Now, Sis, look." He sat up straight in the seat, gazing at the street as they rode along, seemingly interested only in the trees, the houses, the people waiting to cross. "You know they are a family of kooks. That *we* are a family of kooks. All but you. You're normal, and your family is. So normal that, in my book, you are simply wonderful! Your home, your friends—each one of you. Alison, the busy doctor, interested in his hospital, his patients, interested, too, in the school board and the fire department. The way Susan does her summer job as lifeguard and is interested in the little bugs on the flowers. You—all wrapped up in whether Carol gets a little silly or whether Susan puts on the right blouse with the right skirt, whether you should bake beans or make spaghetti . . .

"Your beautiful house, and the dog and the cat, and the salt block for any stray wild animals that come in from the woods. Your friends—the four doctors, the four wives, the dozen or so normal kids . . . Why, Gene, this headshrinker could live with Addie and Mike for ten years and not hear or see anything like what I've seen in your home the past two days."

"Yes, but—" He had said that he wanted to talk to Alison. *About* the psychiatrist, *about* his problems—not . . .

Shawn Burke nodded and threw his cigarette out of the window. "I know. It's been only two days. But—well—I wanted to reassure this man. When he asked if he could talk to my family, I *had* to say that you, and the doctor, were my family. I had to tell him that, Gene."

The truth— Gene turned the car into the hospital parking lot. Shawn said things about the modern building and all the cars.

Gene was worried. Very worried. She had worked hard and long for that normalcy he spoke of, in her home, in her family. And she was beginning to think that she had worked successfully. Even Carol was coming out of her childish fears, her moods, her emotional turbulence. Gene could plan on the future—she had thought she could.

And that future was going to be "normal," too. School for the girls, trips for the four of them during vacations, the girls settling into careers—Carol to teach kindergarten, Susan to be a lab worker—or they would marry.

But now, to have all this invaded, perhaps threatened . . .

The hospital was, indeed, a handsome, modern building. It was, also, busy. Gene led the way up the ramp to the door—the emergency room was closed, and no light bloomed above its doors. Going into the hospital corridor, nurses moved about; an orderly was taking the cart somewhere. A patient in a drooping bathrobe shuffled along the shining floor; the babies in Maternity were crying up a storm. There were only a few outsiders in evidence at this hour, a detail man swinging his heavy satchel, the mother or wife waiting outside a patient's room and pacing the floor —ten steps one way, ten steps back.

A pan clanged, a bell rang, and Dr. Libby Gillis came swinging toward them, her dark hair alive, her friendly smile wide.

"Hello!" she greeted Gene, her eyes sliding to Shawn. "How are you?"

59

"I'm fine," said Gene, moving on, her hand smoothing her skirt over her hips. If she could ever look so slim, so well-groomed, so smart, even in a white hospital coat . . .

If she could ever speak in such a clear, assured voice and be so *alive* in the way she walked . . .

She looked around. Shawn had stopped in the middle of the hall and was gazing back at Dr. Gillis who, by now, was at the far end of the corridor and going into a patient's room. He shook his head, turned, and grinned at Gene.

"Isn't she something?" he demanded boyishly.

Gene nodded. "She really is," she said, her tone patient.

Shawn walked toward her. "You know?" he said. "If I wasn't bound to be a priest—maybe—just maybe—"

"Oh, be still!" said Gene sharply.

The man's head tilted inquiringly. "It's only my personal decision," he reminded his sister, "that celibacy is required. . . ."

Gene did not answer him. Her head up, her cheeks pink, she walked swiftly to the desk and said that she and Mr. Burke were supposed to meet Dr. Cornel.

"Yes, Mrs. Cornel," said the pretty girl properly. Her eyes slid curiously toward Shawn. "Doctor said to ask you to wait in the Board Room. Please?"

"Thank you." Gene turned on her heel and walked down the hall, Shawn amiably following her.

The Board Room was in meticulous order, the chairs neatly set about the table. The windows looked out upon the front lawn of the hospital. Sprinklers waved lazy, silver streams across the grass and the borders of white petunias and blue ageratum. But there was an air of waiting and suspense in the quiet room.

Gene left the door open and took a chair with her back to the light. She could watch the door, look out into the corridor. Shawn roamed about the room, examined a picture on the wall and the framed charter of the hospital. He went to the window and played with the cord of the blind. Now he

60

did not smile. His lips were drawn tightly in against his teeth; his hand was clenched. From time to time Gene glanced at him, not speaking. What could she *say?*

She watched the door. The cart went past, a man upon it; a nurse carrying an I.V. bottle was with it. Two nurses walked fast in the opposite direction—someone laughed and broke it off abruptly. A bell rang, another one—a man's voice rose too far away to have his words distinguishable. A Gray Lady came along carrying two pots of flowers. They were heavy, and Gene made an involuntary gesture to help her, remembered where she was, and why, and sat back again in her chair.

And finally, after what seemed a long time, Alison came in, his step soundless. As always in the hospital, he was in spotless white. Shoes, duck trousers, T shirt, long white coat. His face and his bald head were pinkly clean. He smiled at his wife, glanced at Shawn. He was a tall man, with an air of authority. Gene sighed and looked down at her hands in her lap. Alison would take over now.

"Shawn," he said crisply, "you won't be needed here."

Gene's head lifted.

"*Ho!*" cried Shawn, swinging around. "You're going to talk *about* me!"

Gene's face crumpled with distress. Alison glanced at her, but he spoke, and calmly, to Shawn. "Yes, of course we are," he said readily. "Look. Why don't you take Gene's car—or better still, you might go down to the beach with Dr. Gillis. She's off duty for the rest of the day, and at lunch I heard her say she was going down there."

"That the tall, dark-haired doctor, female type?" Shawn asked, walking fast toward the door.

Alison nodded, watching him.

"That's for me!" declared Shawn. "Where do I find her?"

"I'll take you," said Alison quietly. As he passed his wife, his hand lay for a second, warmly, on Gene's shoulder.

He was gone for ten minutes, and Gene waited tensely.

When Alison returned she was standing at the window and ready to whirl on him.

"Why did you do a thing like that?" she demanded. "That woman—"

Alison carefully closed the door into the hall.

"That woman," he said softly, "is a nice, friendly girl."

Gene nodded. "Yes. Friendly! With everybody! Bill Sims—Frank McManus—Howard Copeland—Willard Laurent and Colonel Ross—but especially with Dewey Windsor!"

"Oh, Gene." Alison came to her side.

She looked up at him, then she sobbed sharply and pressed her face to his shoulder. "I'm scared, Alison," she said in a muffled tone.

He patted her arm. "Yes," he agreed, "I know you are scared. But not about Libby Gillis."

Gene gulped, sniffled, and looked up at Alison; her finger dabbed at her eye. "What then? Shawn?"

Alison smiled and took her elbow. "Let's go over to my office," he said.

But Gene was not ready to be guided.

"Dr. Bailey is waiting for us over there," Alison explained. "He wants to talk to you."

Gene leaned toward him. "To *us*," she amended.

"All right," Alison agreed. "To us."

To Shawn's "family," thought Gene, walking toward the door.

The clinic at Bayard was composed of two small buildings separated by a covered passageway that led to the hospital. In each building was a double suite of doctors' offices and a common waiting room. It was possible, as Dr. Cornel chose to do that day, to enter a doctor's office without going through the waiting room. Thus he led Gene directly into his office and consultation room, where they encountered the tall, dark man who was the psychiatrist, Dr. Bailey.

The room was quiet, restful—green tiled floor, creamy gauze curtains, bleached-wood furniture. The air conditioning shut out the day's heat. Sounds came only dimly from outside. Gene stood within the door and gazed at Dr. Bailey, her gloved hands twisting together. Slightly tousled red hair, her full-skirted blue dress, her anxious, puzzled face—she looked younger than Susan.

Dr. Bailey was tall, very tall. And dark. His hair was black and thick upon his head; his eyes were dark and deeply set. His cheeks showed deep hollows. He wore a suit of dark-gray flannel, faintly pin-striped. His tie was dark blue, with a single diagonal stripe of white, bordered thinly by light blue. He stood, one hand on the back of the chair he had occupied, the other on his hip, and he looked at Gene Cornel.

She tried to smile, then she looked up and around at her husband. "You'll stay with me, Alison!" she cried.

"Yes," he assured her. "Unless . . ."

She sighed and moved toward a chair. A surgeon's wife, she knew about that "unless."

"But," Alison reminded her, "that might bring Dr. Gillis back, too."

Now Gene could manage a faint smile, and she could acknowledge the introduction to Dr. Bailey with some dignity. She managed to say a few gracious things about the famous clinic in Kansas where he was on the staff.

He acknowledged her amenities, then he sat down and turned his chair to face her. Alison took his chair behind the desk and tipped it back, his face alert, but evidently he meant to be only a listener.

Dr. Bailey's voice was like soft, short fur, pleasant as it touched the ear, and warmly reassuring. He used almost no gestures as he talked—the whole flow of his conversation was toward Gene and what she had to tell him. He asked her about herself, her education.

She had been an R.N.

Had she worked after her marriage?

"I became pregnant almost at once. Then the war was going on, and my husband went to Europe—I had a second

63

baby before he came back."

"That was difficult?"

"Oh, I had company. Lots of women managed to get along under those circumstances. Of course Carol didn't know her father, and Susan didn't. When he did come home, he was a stranger."

Dr. Bailey asked about the girls now—their interests, hers.

"I keep house—not very well. I'm untidy. But I keep trying. I work with the flowers in our yard. I—well—" She looked up into the intent eyes of the doctor.

"Look," she said sharply, "are you psychoanalyzing me?"

Dr. Bailey laughed, and so did Alison.

"Calm down, Gene," he said gently.

"But—he—"

"I am very interested in Mr. Burke's background," said Dr. Bailey.

"But that's just the point," said Gene. She laid her small purse on the desk and leaned toward the psychiatrist. "I'm not, really. Not his background, I mean. I've hardly seen my brother since my marriage—and before that. I've not been with him, or around him, for years!"

Dr. Bailey took the announcement calmly. "Yes," he said quietly.

"I know that Shawn gave me as his family, that he wanted —well, he told you that, but—"

"I understand," said Dr. Bailey.

"*Do* you?" Gene asked, again tense, and visibly worried.

"Look." Alison dropped his chair and leaned toward his wife. "Dr. Bailey, Gene, is a skilled psychiatrist, world-recognized . . ."

"I know who he is," said Gene, with dignity. "I know that the eastern psychiatrists brought him into Shawn's case because he is so very able."

Alison shrugged and leaned back again. Dr. Bailey smiled at the small woman in blue. He then took up, from beside his chair, a leather folder, unzipped its sides, and laid the thing open on the leaf of Alison's desk. As he talked, his fingers lifted and turned the papers ring-bound within it.

"Shawn Burke," he said slowly, "is a handsome and a brilliant young man." He turned a page over. "His grades in college were at the top of his class. True, he delayed going to the university until he was thirty or so, but his work there was excellent. He took his master's degree and earned a teaching fellowship in political science. He did teach for a year, noted for his appeal to the students, as well as for his advanced ideas."

Another sheet was turned. "Instead of teaching a second year, or working further toward his doctorate, Mr. Burke then had this vocation for the church."

Gene opened her lips to speak, then shook her head. "Go on," she said.

"I'll gladly answer any questions."

"Yes. But I shouldn't have interrupted."

"This meeting, Mrs. Cornel, should be a means for helping you as much as me. But—the questions can come later. I'll go on with Shawn's record. He had this vocation—and as is routine before being admitted to the seminary, he underwent various psychiatric testings. These examinations are required, and they are designed not so much to keep the neurotics out as to help them once they get in. Shawn's test results were not entirely satisfactory, if one takes adjustment as a criterion, but today we find a great many young people who think they are called upon to change the world.

"After a conference of some length, the authorities decided to let Shawn Burke try the thing. For a year at least. It has been found that psychological testing is valuable in assessing future ministers. Any mental ill-adjustment which is revealed can be treated by a competent Christian psychiatrist and often is turned to useful ministerial ends.

"With a young man like Burke, the ministry is found to be good therapy. Sometimes the deep need that impelled these men to seek the ministry often has a balancing effect on a disturbed personality. The examining doctors were ready to see what the prospects for Mr. Burke would seem to be."

"They had decided that he was neurotic," said Gene quietly.

"Oh, yes! Definitely. And then, as you may or may not know, last winter he suffered a nervous breakdown."

Gene's head lifted. "But that's what Ginny said!" she cried.

Dr. Bailey looked at her, a question in his face.

"Nan told me," she explained. "The wives talked about my brother this morning—down on the beach. I wasn't there, of course. We often go there for an hour or so—it's so nice by the river—but I was busy. Anyway, Ginny said that she thought Shawn must have had a nervous break-down. They'd all met him yesterday, you see, and—well, we always talk things over."

Alison stirred in his chair. "It might be difficult, and certainly would be lengthy," he told the puzzled psychiatrist, "to explain the 'wives' to you, Doctor."

Dr. Bailey sat back in his chair. "You might try," he suggested.

"Should I?"

"Yes. I think the effort might be very worth while."

Dr. Cornel looked at his wife. She waved her hand a little, indicating that he should speak. She still thought that Dr. Bailey was studying her. But she could manage to sit quietly while Alison talked.

"I'll make this as brief as I can," said the big doctor in white. "Though there's a good bit of material. The 'wives,' you see, are the women who are married to the four men on the staff of Bayard Hospital and Clinic. They, perforce, are united, just as we are, by our association.

"We came here to Bayard together—three of us did. Dr. Shelton came later. But Dr. Ruble, Dr. Windsor, and I came here after the war. Then Dr. Kurt Lillard was the fourth doctor. His father, also a doctor, had built the hospital and clinic. We were, all of us, fresh from war service. We put our savings into the project, and that left us all broke, except Lillard whose father was rich.

"We came here together with our wives. We hunted for places to live—together. Hunted them together, I mean, and right after the war such places were scarce and inadequate. Two of us had small children. Perforce the wives helped each other.

"There never has been a formal 'organization' among them. But those first days they house-hunted, and compared notes, and helped each other make do until plans could be made to buy or build our own dwelling places. I remember that the Rubles stayed in a motel—not a modern, up-to-date one. The baby was in a basket, and Bob and Ginny and little Mary slept in the one bed. Gene and I rented a house that had no cabinets in the kitchen."

"And twelve-foot ceilings," said Gene bitterly. "Three tiny closets in the whole house!"

"That's right. But it also had a yard where Ginny could bring her children to play with ours."

"Hazel and Dewey Windsor bought a lot," said Gene.

"Yes. A beautiful, wooded lot. They had a house plan and then found that they could not get the needed GI loan to finance a custom-built house. So they sold the lot and bought a new house built by a lumber yard. It was the usual one—no dining room, but a big picture window, one bedroom, and a plastic-tiled bath. Since, they have added to it and now have a beautiful home. The Windsors have no children."

"But she helps us raise ours," said Gene, laughing a little. "Hazel does."

"We—they—the wives—all help each other. They have been, from the first, good friends. They talk frankly and display understanding.

"When Kurt Lillard ran into some—er—difficulties"— Alison glanced at Gene, who nodded. He need say little more about that bad time—"and decided to leave Bayard,

Garde Shelton came in. He married a local girl, and she immediately took her place in the organization of wives."

"The husbands, too," Gene spoke up. She looked at Dr. Bailey. "We do things together. The men built the Windsor patio. We all helped plaster and paint the farmhouse which the Rubles bought to remodel."

"My back has never been the same since," Alison contributed. "But we did—we do—things together. Gene's right. We laid carpet squares in the Rubles' family room and started their pool. Fortunately Bob called in a contractor to get the thing finished. When we built our home—four years ago—everyone helped. With advice, labor—"

Gene laughed. "Alison bought everything through the hospital, to save money, you see. He contracted the labor. And as often as not, nails, hinges, and stuff would be dropped at the hospital, then one of us—often as not one of us *wives* —would need to pick some needed thing up and bring it to the contractor on the site. Ginny, I remember, decided that it was easier to drive with a keg of nails in the back of her station wagon."

"When we added to the hospital," said Alison, "it was the wives, as a group, who told us to go ahead with it. They would give up the trips planned for the next two years and economize in various ways."

"And do you know," Gene asked the attentive visitor, "then these birds wouldn't let us have one word to say about how the additional features should go?"

"We heard about that, and still do," Alison agreed. "Ours —theirs—isn't all sweetness and light, Doctor. The women argue just about as fiercely as they love one another. Nan Shelton says it was not only she having her two babies—it was more a joint project. I expect the younger Ruble children, Sarah and Jan, were the same."

"Sometimes we are wise," said Gene thoughtfully. "Like the time we all four took lessons and really learned to sew. Other times we've been just as foolish—"

"Yes," said her husband. "When you decided to make apple butter out in the yard. Nearly burned up that whole end of the county."

Gene laughed. "I guess there have been more foolish times than wise ones. But the point is—"

"They stick together," said Alison. "And it's a big help —to them and to us doctors. There was the time when our dog warned me of a prowler in our house. I foolishly picked up a gun and almost shot a sixteen-year-old boy. He was mentally disturbed. Things could have been nasty—especially if I had shot him."

"Or if he'd got to the girls' room," said Gene soberly.

"Yes. The town was pretty well upset when we—I—saw to it that he was confined. But our wives weathered that, and most remarkable, they didn't let themselves, or the hospital, get involved in any town quarreling about it."

"We help each other in big ways, too," said Gene. "Garde Shelton has done wonders for Carol, our older daughter. Garde is a pediatrician—and he really understands young people."

"I guess the main contribution," said Alison thoughtfully, "has been the way the wives protect our position in the town. I need not tell you that doctors as a class are vulnerable. But our wives do cover for us. They don't gossip. They see that our children behave themselves. They themselves are respected in the community, for appearance, behavior, and performance." He glanced at his wife and laughed a little.

"I can see that my words are going to be fed back to me," he said. "But it is true. Also, they permit, and encourage, us men to take our part in community affairs. They don't always like it—but when Gene decided that being on the school board was taking too many of my evenings, I am sure it was the other wives who persuaded her that my service was desirable.

"They serve—their meetings do—as a clearinghouse for problems, for troubles—and for pleasures, too. All of which adds up to a lengthy explanation to you, only to tell you why Ginny Ruble suspected—though it was certain to be a non-clinical opinion—that Shawn had had a breakdown. . . .

"It explains, too, why Nan called and told Gene what had been said. With them, with us, no one has a trouble, or a problem, that does not belong to the group. Perhaps she called Gene out of sympathy, perhaps as a warning—but certainly she wanted Gene to know what had been said. Have I thoroughly confused you, Doctor?"

Dr. Bailey slowly shook his head, a faint smile about his eyes and lips. He had been very interested, and while the Cornels talked he had watched them closely, husband and wife. Now he nodded and laid his pen down on his opened notebook. He sat back in his chair.

"I think," he began, his gaze upon Gene, "that we need no further preliminary discussion. I think I understand the situation here, and I feel you should know now, Mrs. Cornel, that it is feared your brother is in a stage of rapidly advancing schizophrenia."

He spoke gently, but Gene stared at him, unbelieving. Then her eyes went in alarm to Alison's face. She was white, and she began to tremble. He got up from his chair and went around to her, put his hand on her shoulder. She looked up at him.

"You *knew?*" she asked.

"Yes."

"But why didn't you tell me?"

"I thought Dr. Bailey could do it better. That you wouldn't —fight—him."

Gene's head drooped. Then slowly she lifted it, her lips pressed together. "All right," she said harshly. "Then *do* tell me! Exactly what has happened to us? When did this thing begin to show itself? Why should it have developed? What can we expect?"

"Mrs. Cornel," said Dr. Bailey quietly, "you, too, should be a doctor."

70

A deep, shuddering sob shook Gene, but she put aside her husband's efforts to lift her from her chair. "I'll be all right," she promised.

For another minute Alison stood beside her; both men watched her, concerned.

"I believe you may go on, Doctor," Alison said then.

Dr. Bailey took still another minute to go back to his records; he picked up his pencil, read the opened page, turned it, read the next one. Then he looked at Gene. She was sitting quietly, the color drained from her face, her hands clasped agonizingly in her lap. But she was calm.

"You asked me when," he said quietly, "how and when —what to expect. I can answer some of your questions now. Others must be speculated upon, then await further observation and examination. For now—

"As I told you, your brother's psychiatric tests before entering seminary were not satisfactory. They showed bad adjustments, erratic protests—various unstable tendencies. Last winter he had this breakdown, and perhaps it was due to the pressures of his religious zeal. One might even speak of it as an extravagant zeal.

"Maybe his unnecessary self-denial of physical outlets to his over-tense emotions could be the reason for his collapse. He did—well—flagellate himself, you know. He fasted. He isolated himself—things like that."

He glanced at Gene. She sat, waiting.

I'll have this man talk to Carol, she was promising herself tensely. *Before he leaves town. Alison can't deny me that!*

"Mrs. Cornel?" asked Dr. Bailey.

She took a deep breath. "I'm listening."

She would make herself think of something else. Of Shawn—down on the sunny beach—with Libby Gillis. The lapping water of the river, the children playing with beach balls, the boats, the handsome woman in her green bathing suit and silvery-petaled swim cap. Shawn—big— young—the golden hair upon his arms—his legs.

71

Schizophrenia!

What if he—suddenly—?

What if, these past three days, Shawn had—?

Gene suppressed the shudder that threatened to tear and twist her. She wove her fingers tightly together and looked at Dr. Bailey's shoulder, not into his deep, all-seeing eyes.

He was talking—though he had paused to watch her. "I believe that the reasons for Mr. Burke's condition go deeper than the emotional strains of his vocation," he said. "*We* believe. A team of capable men evaluated the situation, then the case was referred to our foundation. Certainly we are none of us going to proceed entirely on our 'beliefs.' But we have certain facts. One of them, the largest one, is that trouble now is present. Another is that your brother needs hospitalization, observation, and care.

"From stage three on, almost all mental illness is likely to require some hospitalization. We—our group—refuse to dismiss any condition as hopeless, but—"

"What," Gene asked, her voice hoarse, "what will you do?"

"Oh," said Dr. Bailey in a matter-of-fact tone, "under exceptionally expert direction, our psychiatrists use everything from a pat on the head to drugs. We use talk-it-out therapy and all-out psychoanalysis as well. But only rarely —*very* rarely—do we use insulin or electric shock."

Gene sighed, and both doctors saw her do it.

Dr. Bailey turned the pages of his record. "Here is mentioned his religious zeal," he said slowly, "but personally I do not feel that the real reason behind Burke's condition appears in this clinical report, exhaustive as it is.

"Perhaps you can help us find better, deeper reasons, Mrs. Cornel. Schizophrenia is a deep-rooted trouble, and I will say now that in some cases it is reversible. And that its establishment is not induced by a temporary or a new emotion. Not generally. So could you tell me if this trouble might be traceable to any of Shawn's ancestors?"

72

Gene's head lifted, and the doctor spoke quickly. "Would there have been an aunt, perhaps, who became depressive at the time of menopause? Maybe a grand-uncle who was unmanageable? Families, *you* know—"

Gene's hand clutched at her throat. She sprang to her feet, terrified. *Carol!* They were talking, not about Shawn, but about Carol. The girl was hypersensitive—withdrawn. She quickly felt and showed resentment.

Gene whirled on the two men who were watching her anxiously. "You're talking nonsense!" she cried, her voice shrill. "You don't have to go back to any foolish aunt or temperish uncle. The whole trouble lies in Shawn's own home! If you only knew the family and the household where that boy grew up! *I* know! *I* could tell you!"

But it wouldn't have touched Carol. She had protected her girls!

Dr. Bailey's face did not change. "*Will* you tell me," he said gravely, "about Shawn's home and family?"

Gene's head went back. "No!" she cried. "No, I won't! I—can't! But it's there! And—I'll tell Alison. What he doesn't already know. *He* can talk to you!"

"Do you fear me, Mrs. Cornel?"

"I don't know you. That's all it is. But—you can tell me about Shawn, of course. His—illness. He's the youngest, you know. The baby of the family, he was. And he was a handsome, clever little boy. Very dear. I—I have not known much about him since he was ten. It seems incredible, or would seem that—if I didn't know . . .

"It isn't that I don't believe you, Dr. Bailey! I don't mean to be rude. I—well—there's this: if what you fear is true, if his mind is gone—or his control—don't you think . . . ?"

Dr. Bailey nodded. "Yes. He must be confined. For his sake. And the safety of others. We'll examine him, observe him, perhaps treat him. If there is schizophrenia, perhaps he will respond to drugs and other new treatments. Two out of three patients do respond and can be dismissed after

73

six months or so. If he isn't one of that group, his stay will be—longer."

"When will you know—about him?"

"A month, perhaps. Six weeks—three months. It depends, Mrs. Cornel. Mental illness is not always too clearly defined."

"You'll let—us—know?"

"Of course. I'll be in contact with Dr. Cornel."

"Yes." Not me, she thought. I'd fly to pieces like an old haystack in a high wind. These men know that. . . .

She stood, very white and very brave. "Should I . . .?" she began. "What should I tell my children? They are—old enough—to need to be told—something."

Now Dr. Bailey smiled. He should smile more often, thought Gene. His eyes *glow;* his whole face lights up.

"You're worried about their future," he said. "And quite understandably. But if you are right, and environment, not inheritance, is the root of your brother's trouble, you need not fear an inheritance of any taint in your children. An environmental problem, you know—some emotional trauma, repression or insecurity can be even more important in these cases than heredity."

Gene sighed and her shoulders dropped. Then she looked up again at the tall men. "But I have a daughter . . . " she said tensely.

"Gene," said Alison warningly.

"I must ask him!" Gene told her husband. "I *must*, Alison!"

He lifted his shoulders and threw out his hands in a gesture of surrender.

"You see"—Gene turned back to the psychiatrist—"our older daughter, Carol, is a very high-strung girl. She used to be worse than she is now. Garde Shelton has helped her, but at times she still goes off by herself; she gets too excited. Emotional."

"How old is she?" Dr. Bailey asked his question of Alison. And the doctor answered. Gene, he said, thought the girl felt rejected because they had left her with friends for a month when she wasn't more than eighteen months old. Also, Gene had rigid ideas of behavior, rigid ideas of what the girls should do for amusement, for cultural improvement. She was an overly conscientious mother.

"You get that way if your own mother hasn't given a damn about *your* future!" Gene put in bitterly.

"I don't think Carol feels rejected," Alison told the other doctor. "I don't think there is any sibling jealousy—but Shelton thinks, and I agree with him, that Gene is, and has always been, jealous of Carol. She knows this, subconsciously, feels guilty about it, and tries extra hard to do the right thing for the poor girl."

Gene stared at her husband as if she had never seen this man before. "Where did you ever get such an idea?" she demanded. "Have you always thought I—"

"I've suspected it from the time Carol was six weeks old," he told her calmly. "It wasn't hard to detect. You showed your feeling."

"I did not!"

"You did. You have. To Carol, especially."

"You haven't said a word."

"Would you have listened?"

Gene stood, stunned. "No," she admitted. "I suppose not."

She walked the length of the room and came back. "I suppose you really are analyzing me now," she said ruefully to Dr. Bailey.

"Mrs. Cornel, I—"

"I'm all crawly to think that Alison has felt this way—for eighteen years. I thought he loved me, and—well, maybe not *admired*—but that he was loyal—"

"Gene!" Alison shouted her name. "I do love you. Yes, and admire you, too. I've fought you all the way over Carol. You know I have. I've urged you to let her alone a little."

"I owed her every single thing I have done for her!"

"You've owed her only love and safety."

"But—if you thought I was jealous . . . Oh, that idea is just too much! To be jealous of my own child!"

"It's nothing to be ashamed of, Mrs. Cornel," said Dr. Bailey.

"Isn't it? Why not?"

"Because you didn't feel so deliberately."

"No-o, I didn't. And lately—maybe I'm not jealous any more. We get along better. Garde—he has helped Carol. Did he help me, too? He's talked to me sometimes. About her, you know. He made me let her give up her music lessons. He made me let her learn to drive the car—and date. A little. He insisted that we let her go away to college. And I suppose he was right.

"But just the same—" She walked to the window, her back to the men. "To be jealous . . ." she mourned. "Why should I have such a feeling?"

"Can't you think?" asked Dr. Bailey's deep, soft voice. "Don't you know?"

Gene did not turn. "I didn't—I haven't felt this way about Susan. Have I? Then—you mean, it was only my first child . . . ?"

"Carol was your first child."

"Yes. And I remember—when Alison was at home—that was during the war, and our times together were few and short—I remember resenting it if the baby cried in the night and I would have to attend to her. Before he went overseas, I insisted on taking that trip—leaving Carol with friends."

"Yes. You wanted him for your own."

"Well, why not?" demanded Gene. "After the family I'd had? Of course I wanted him for my own! I wanted to keep him that way."

"Then you have answered your own questions. Haven't you?"

"Yes. But I am still ashamed."

"There is no need. Things will clear up. Your relations with your daughter—with your husband, too, and with Susan—will now be more relaxed. And certainly, without seeing her, I am sure that Carol's situation is in no way similar to your brother's."

Gene nodded. "I can see that, too. And I'm not going to worry about it. I'm not even going to worry about Shawn. You see, our family—his and mine—they did teach me one thing. Not to look ahead. And once I stopped doing that, I stopped being afraid. So—" She walked over to the desk and picked up her purse.

"May I go home now?" she asked politely.

Alison hugged her shoulders. "Yes. You've had a long afternoon." He walked with her to the door. Gene said a polite good-by to Dr. Bailey.

"But," she asked him, "what about Shawn?"

"Dr. Gillis is driving him to the mental-care center." He looked at his wrist. "They should be halfway there by now."

"But what if . . ."

"I'm sure she and Dewey can take care of him," said Alison firmly.

Gene whirled on him. "She and—! Libby Gillis and *Dewey?*" she cried.

Alison nodded to Dr. Bailey. "She'll be all right now," he assured the doctor. "She's completely back on keel."

Chapter 7

GENE DID NOT LET HERSELF LOOK FORWARD. SHE told herself that she did not, and the telling comforted her. But, even against her will, she did look back. She had to. . . .

Hazel, she knew, was upset about the trip to Topeka. Dewey had not got home until five on Tuesday morning!

Eighteen hours riding around with Dr. Gillis was just too much!

She was having a fit. Gene saw and heard some of it for herself. Ginny and Nan had told her the rest.

"We keep reminding her that they were taking a patient—"

"All she says is that it does not take both Dewey and Libby to escort a patient."

The women also reminded Dewey's wife that the "patient" was Gene's brother.

"Are you suggesting that our families get special treatment?"

"In this case, yes, Hazel. The man was sick. It seems he had recently had a nervous breakdown. A doctor was needed in case—well, in case he became excited—or ill—"

"And another M.D. to drive?"

"Well, they spelled each other."

"There are ambulances, aren't there?"

"I expect the men had reasons not to use an ambulance."

"I don't care what their reasons are or were. I do not like the idea of my husband driving three or four hundred miles, and back, with that woman."

"Oh, Hazel!"

"You wouldn't like it, in my place!"

"No. But for Gene's brother—"

It was at this point, reached several times in her friends' efforts to "talk to" Hazel, that Gene decided she must tell the others something of the reasons behind that trip to Topeka, started in the guise of a drive on a pleasant summer afternoon, continued as a reasonable suggestion made by one of the doctors.

"He was emotionally unstable. You see, he's been sick. And he is a big man. Dewey was needed should some sort of force have been required."

"And Libby?"

"She was the decoy; she persuaded him to start the trip.

There may have been better ways, Hazel. The men, and Dr. Bailey, thought this way might work. And it evidently did."

"Alison planned to be the one to go," said Nan. "But he had to stay with Gene."

"Yes," said Gene. "I wanted him with me. And said so. I didn't know about the trip to Topeka, of course. Not then."

"That's right," said Ginny Ruble. "With Alison out, Dewey seemed to be the one most able to go. Bob had three terms, and Garde is swamped with a measles epidemic."

"Chicken pox," Nan corrected her.

"Well, something that keeps him on the run. Anyway, Dewey had to go—and you should be more reasonable about it, Hazel."

"I'm not going to be reasonable at all. They took eighteen hours for that drive together. And you can't tell me they didn't enjoy it!"

There was nothing anyone could think of to say about that.

Gene talked to her daughters, but not in detail. Details might come out later, but for now it would be enough . . .

That morning she asked Carol and Susan to drive over beyond Plover with her for strawberries.

"Pick them?" asked Susan suspiciously.

"They're cheaper that way."

"It's hard work, Mom. In the sun . . ."

"Yes. And very good for the figure you're putting on," said Gene tartly. "But—we'll see. If the berries are reasonable, I'll let you off from picking. But I shall expect help in getting them ready to freeze."

"O. K. It's a deal."

So they started out, in the quiet freshness of the early morning. Susan crawled into the back seat, saying that she meant to get the rest of her sleep.

Carol sat beside her mother, her face quiet. Now and then Gene would glance at the girl, neat as a pin, her white blouse crisp, her gray denim shorts fitting well, her white sneakers clean. Gene ineffectually tried to conceal her own battered sandals and wondered if she actually was jealous of Carol?

Ye-es. She decided that she was. A little. Of the girl's style, maybe—and, lately, of her poise. These things Gene did not have. And probably could not acquire.

"I should have done something about my hair," she murmured unhappily.

"You're all right," said Carol.

"You combed yours."

"Yes, I know. But, Mom—"

"Mhmmmn?"

"People like you the way you are."

Gene smiled, then thought about that statement for the next three miles. People did like her. And Carol did not make friends quickly; she was uneasy with groups, or with strangers.

"Maybe we should work on each other," Gene suggested.

Carol glanced at her, startled.

"I mean," said Gene, "*you* could remind me to comb my hair. I could, maybe, help you to get along with people. That would be harder . . ."

"I don't know. When you think you are in a hurry . . ."

Gene nodded. "We'll try. Both of us."

"Won't I learn to like people when I get away to school?"

Was that what the girl was hoping? Well, she might . . . In their house, noisy Susan, big masterful Alison, and fussy, fidgeting Gene—probably Carol had had to move into the background. . . .

Gene sighed. "I thought I'd talk a little about your uncle Shawn," she said.

"*Yip!*" said Susan, bouncing forward to put her head over the seat back, between Carol and Gene. "Daddy said we were not to pester you about him."

Gene bit her lip. "What else did he tell you?"

"Nothing. Just that he had left—and we could see *that!*

And he said that we were not to pester you. What happened, Mom? Did you have a fight?"

"Oh, Susan, don't be ridiculous. You knew that I was to take him to the hospital . . ."

"Ye-es. Why?"

"He was sick."

"He didn't look sick."

"You're no judge. The doctors thought he was sick. And they sent him on to another hospital."

"What kind of sick, Mom?" Carol asked. While Susan talked, she had been thinking.

"He had been studying very hard at the seminary," said Gene. "He became ill last spring—and he didn't get over it. That's why he came to visit us. To let Alison see what could be done for him. Your father, I mean."

The girls exchanged smiles.

Gene turned the car into the road which would lead to the farm where strawberries might be available.

"How was he sick, Mom?" Carol asked again.

"His nerves. His ability to concentrate—to stay in school."

"Did he—does he know he is sick?" Her face was anxious.

"Why—I don't know, Carol. Not particularly, I mean. Of course he came to talk to your father. But he didn't mention his—illness—to me."

"Daddy says he is a very smart man. Brilliant."

"Yes. Shawn is smart."

Carol sighed. "Then I guess he knows he is sick."

Gene drove into the farmyard. "Your father and the specialist who saw him think he will be helped where he is. Now—stay in the car until I talk to Mr. Stelljes. He looks busy."

Again the girls exchanged amused glances.

Gene stepped out of the car. "All right!" she told them. "I suppose I'll always think of you as being about six!"

"Poor Mom," said Carol, watching her walk over to the open shed where the farmer was directing a couple of women who were putting strawberries into boxes and talking simultaneously to the customers who had arrived before Gene.

Gene bought so many strawberries that she decided to make sun preserves with some of them. Ginny must be called over to show her exactly how. Nan and Hazel came, too.

For an hour they worked in the kitchen, then they took the pans out to the sunny terrace and covered them with glass. They must chain the boxer and keep the cat in the house.

"I can see, after all your precautions," said Ginny, "the way Alison will come charging out here this evening and tip over one or all of the pans."

Gene laughed. "He'll do that," she predicted. "Now, come back to the porch. I'll fix us something cool."

The porch was the best part of the Cornel house, many of their friends thought. It was a big, square room, with louvered windows, comfortable furniture, a view of the valley and the river, a fireplace for winter days.

Gene made iced coffee and brought it and a plate of cookies to her friends.

"I thought I'd tell you something about Shawn," she said abruptly.

Ginny looked warningly at Hazel.

"She'll stop being mad at Dewey," Gene assured them, "when I tell you that he—my brother—was taken to a psychiatric clinic."

"We knew that," Hazel told her.

Gene looked around, her cheeks red."You did?"

"Sure. What else is in Topeka?"

Gene sat down on the end of the chaise which Ginny occupied. Ginny was tiny—there was plenty of room. "I didn't know . . ." she said unhappily.

"Our dear husbands haven't said a word to us," Nan assured her. "And we don't really *know* anything."

"No. I guess not. But—well, his trouble is mental. Psychotic is the word used now, I believe. Neuroses. Psychoses. They all mean the same thing. He's broken down—mentally. And he needs to be under observation and treatment until the doctors know—"

She looked around at her friends. "Oh," she cried desperately, "I hate this! I hate this happening to us!"

"Gene, dear—" said Nan.

Gene gulped and drank some of her coffee, choking on it, then coughing. Her eyes were red. "He's very sick," she blurted. "But Dr. Bailey said he didn't think there was much chance of the cause being inherent. He—I—think the whole thing was caused by the trouble in our home. By the sort of woman my mother is!"

For a long minute she sat staring straight ahead of her, and no one wanted to speak. The ringing telephone was a great relief. When Gene came back, Shawn was not mentioned again.

For the following days nothing was said to Gene about her brother. Almost as carefully, the other wives did not discuss the matter with each other. They were sorry for Gene—Shawn had seemed to be a very likable young man—but discussion was not possible. Just then. For a time.

To everyone's relief, Hazel stopped talking about the trip to Topeka.

The families did the usual things of early summer. They gathered at the club, on the deck of the Shelton house for an impromptu supper; they helped Bob Ruble decide on a new riding lawn mower and discussed the new style of women, for evening parties, putting on floor-length skirts of almost any material wrapped tightly about their waists.

Both the men and the women discussed these things. Hazel had tried one of the skirts, liked the way it looked— "But it got in my way when I went to cook the hot dogs."

Shawn was not mentioned. Libby Gillis was ignored.

Until . . .

On Tuesday afternoons, winter and summer, there was a women's luncheon and bridge party at the club. These were variously attended, and the wives often let weeks pass without going near. Then some reason, in this case their consciences, made them decide that they should attend. After all, they had helped organize the club.

"But I'm never ready to dress up at twelve o'clock on Tuesday morning," protested Ginny Ruble.

"Oh, you could be. Probably be good for you, too."

"I play terrible bridge."

"I've not met up with any champions on the veranda."

"Oh, Hazel!"

But they would go—for a week or two. They went that next Tuesday, Gene coming in late and breathless. The lunch was good—wafer-thin ham, new peas, delicious crisp rolls.

Nan wore a new suit of sheer navy blue, piped in white.

"It's beautiful!" cried Ginny.

"I bought it to go to the convocation in Virginia this spring," said Nan. "Then the youngest Kibbler boy got that awful ear infection and Garde didn't go."

"And you haven't worn it to church because you sing in the choir."

"That's right. Summer clothes—here in Bayard—"

"Shorts," Ginny agreed. "Gingham dresses. I never need anything else. Except for church."

"And parties," Gene reminded her. "The Saturday-night dances here—"

"That's different. But even then we wear the same old things, unless something special is on deck."

"Something special like Libby Gillis?" asked Ruth Kibbler, laughing.

"Don't mention that woman's name!" screamed Mabel Ross from the far end of their long table. "I know she is beautiful. I know she is smart. I know all of us women are trying to spruce up and show her some competition, but I do think we might better stop. We just don't have what it takes, girls."

"Takes to do what?" asked someone.

"To break up my home for one," said Mabel glumly.

"Mabel!" said Catherine Sims warningly.

And, indeed, everyone on the porch was listening.

Mabel tossed her head. As nice as a person could be, Mabel was not a beautiful woman. British, married to an Army officer now retired, her idea of clothes was a tweed suit in cold weather, seersucker in the summer. The same suit to be worn everywhere, the same shirtwaist dress. For evening affairs there was the utility crepe.

"It can't be a town secret," this likable person now told the other women, "that she comes out to our place three times a week to ride. Stretch pants, a superlative white shirt . . . Doesn't she do *any* work at the hospital?"

The wives, without so much as a glance at one another, closed their ranks. Ginny buttered a roll; Hazel touched her napkin to her lips and picked up her ice-tea glass. Gene glanced through the window and down to where three boys and a girl strolled along the pier. The girl was Mary Ruble. Nan rearranged her white gloves under her flat blue purse.

"The Colonel says," Mabel was continuing, "that he doesn't ask her out. But who believes him? Anyway, invited or not, she assumes that she is welcome, and she comes. And stays. And the Colonel enjoys her; he rides with her. Certainly she rides well! That woman does everything well!"

Down the table someone said a word or two that the wives could not hear.

"But, my dear woman," said Mabel's strident voice, "haven't you learned that the Gillis type like married men better? They are safer! They are older. They have some money to spend. They can't involve a girl in embarrassing situations, or they think they cannot!

"But do you know? One married man's wife stands ready

to stir up a few embarrassing situations herself! I didn't marry the Colonel and go through the years since with him just to have some long-legged free-lancer step in and enjoy the fruits of my efforts. I mean to show this woman where I stand, and in the process I truly think that the Colonel will see an item or two as well! I—"

The women on the veranda ate their strawberry sherbet and listened to this outraged wife and watched her with fascination and even awe. With expectation, too.

Once Ginny ventured a glance at Hazel; so did Nan. Dewey's wife had been listening, but her expression showed nothing. If it reassured her to hear that Libby Gillis had interests other than Dewey, Hazel was not ready to admit it. Besides, she probably thought that between her husband and Colonel Ross, there was no contest. Hazel did nothing by halves.

Nor did the Rosses, wife or husband. Because, five days after the bridge luncheon—or maybe it was six—anyway, on Monday morning Colonel Ross showed up at the Bayard Hospital and demanded to see Dr. Gillis.

Dr. Gillis, he was told, was in surgery.

"I'll wait."

"I can't promise how long it will be, sir. They are doing major surgery, with another case probable."

"I'll wait."

"Yes, sir."

Colonel Ross waited, but he did not wait quietly. He paced the waiting room; he paced the center hall; he growled at those who spoke to him. He looked at his watch and at the clock.

He was an impressive figure, this retired Army officer, a big man, ramrod straight, with a guardsman's step and an impressive scowl. He upset things in the front hall of Bayard Hospital just by being there.

And the hospital was upset enough without him, for that morning it was entertaining what the manager called a stub-

86

born mother.

The case—mother and child—had come to the hospital about eight. The baby was sick and it was immediately determined that he had a hernia, strangulated. At once Dr. Shelton told the young mother that surgery should be performed. Mentally he was telling himself that if Cornel could put the colostomy back an hour, he would take care of this. *Stat!*

But the girl in the green print dress shook her hair out of her eyes and said unhurriedly that, no, they couldn't operate on Wayne.

Dr. Shelton talked to her. He explained about hernias—ruptures—the baby was already in great distress; he would get worse.

"I cannot decide such a thing without my husband."

Where was her husband?

"At work. He gets off at three."

"But, Mrs. Ewers . . .'"

"We live here close to Bayard—about three miles. We got us ten acres and some stock we're feeding."

"Is your husband at home?"

"No. I told you, he's at work. At Plover."

Garde took a deep breath. The mother—the girl, surely not more than eighteen—was thin; her hair was blond and thick. Her skin was pale. Her dress was clean, but there was a look of struggling poverty about her and the baby.

If her husband worked for the fertilizer plant, the doctor there might have sent the baby to the hospital. He had not. The husband, said the child's mother, didn't care for the plant doctor.

"What does your husband do at the plant?"

"He's a sweeper."

"Yes. We can get word to him," Dr. Shelton planned.

"Oh, no, sir! Don't you go botherin' him at work! The last time I did, he said that he'd about kill me if I ever tried such a thing again."

Garde thought he might have to take that risk.

"And it ain't only him," said the mother. "The company . . . I did try to call him when the sheep got themselves out through the fence and on to the road, and the lady that answers the telephone said an employee—that's one of the men who work in the fertilizin' plant—she said that an *employee* could not be called to the phone except under an emergency!"

"But this is an emergency! Your baby can die before Mr. Ewers gets off at three o'clock."

"Oh?" said the mother, looking sadly at the baby on the table. "That makes things bad, don't it?"

"Yes, it does!" said the big doctor gruffly. "You will either have to take this child to St. Louis or let him be admitted here and cared for, Mrs. Ewers!"

It took quite a bit more talk, but finally Mrs. Ewers consented to have the baby put to bed. "But you don't pick up no knife!" she said sharply. "Until my husband gets here! He'll have the say!"

Garde did some quick mental arithmetic. Nine o'clock—three o'clock—a half-hour drive from Plover. Things could not wait that long!

He told the mother to call the Plover plant and leave a message for her husband to come to the Bayard Hospital as soon as possible.

"He won't git here till three-thirty," said the girl resignedly. "He knows I git excited."

"Meanwhile I'll try to reduce the hernia without surgery."

"You do that, Doctor."

Garde tried. But it was no good. Surgery was their only hope. He gave the baby a mild sedative to reduce the pain and the dangerous crying. He would keep trying to persuade the mother—he'd get Cornel to try . . .

And he would attempt to go on with his other tasks. He even listened to Colonel Ross who waylaid him at the end of the front hall.

But as the man talked, all Dr. Shelton could think of was the mental picture he had of the lady in question, Dr. Gillis, presently seated behind her shield, answering Cornel's demand for "Numbers, please, Libby?"

"One hundred sixty over eighty—and eighty-eight," said in Libby's throaty voice.

Libby, green cap, gauze mask, green robe, in her ear the stethoscopic device through which, at heart level, she kept track of the beat; beside her the respiratory-assister machine keeping up its measured pant. Again she read pressure and pulse—they were steady. Her finger tips pressed the unconscious face of her patient. Libby was at work.

As was Alison Cornel. Dewey, the patient's physician, was with him. All working, all busy. Cornel had delayed going in until nine-twenty, hoping that he could do the Ewers repair first. Now, at work, he was ready for anything the case might show up; the cannulae were ready for blood if they were needed. But he had a good patient—and a very bad case.

Cancer was there, pain on the x-ray films clipped in the shadow box, and proven by biopsy. In the extremity of what he would find, he was ready to construct a colostomy. Now he was working—he would find the tumor; sponges, clamps, ligatures, scissors, all would come to his hand.

He would reach deep to get all of the tumor. He would lift it out, take every precaution, and he could be thankful for a good patient. Again and again he would ask for the numbers—and get them. He would take time to check on the circulating nurse and her count of the sponges. . . .

They were getting through. In another ten minutes they would be through. If, then, Garde could take the baby in . . . That dumb woman! That stupid woman! Her husband *not to be disturbed!*

What was it Ross was saying? Oh, yes. About Libby . . .

From the far end of the hall Bob Ruble was approaching them. He had just made a delivery or was waiting on one.

Shrouded in white, his mask dangling, he came up to the two men and greeted them.

"Soldiering?" he asked pleasantly. "No horses to feed? No tonsils or mumps?"

Again Colonel Ross went over his routine. He had said it all to Garde, that he thought he had a complaint against the hospital, that he wanted that woman out of the way—out of the hospital, out of the town . . .

"Oh, now, look!" protested Dr. Ruble.

"I mean it!" shouted the Colonel.

"Well, let's go in here and talk about it, shall we? A little. Garde and I are both busy, you know." He pushed against the door of the doctors' room. Colonel Ross preceded him, his face flushed, his eyes overly bright.

"There has to be a showdown!" he cried. "Ruble, I am *not* going to break up my home without cause. I—"

"Hey, hey!" cried Bob. "Are you saying you would break up your home over Dr. Gillis? Because it sounds as if you were saying that."

Colonel Ross accepted the cup of coffee which Garde handed him, looked at it curiously, then set it down on the table. He paced the floor. "She's a damned exciting woman!" he declared. "She comes out and rides—and talks. She makes me laugh. And—" He whirled to face the two men on the couch.

"Are you telling me that *you* can't conceive throwing your hat over the windmill for a woman like that?"

He was expecting—demanding—an answer.

"I am pretty well married . . ." Bob told him, his tone mild.

"You are! But you're in your forties."

"Yes. But even so I cannot conceive threatening my present home and family with any woman."

"You can conceive wanting to?"

Bob pursed his lips, then shrugged. "Maybe," he conceded.

"What about you, Shelton?"

"I'll try not to be tempted," said Garde thoughtfully, "and faced with such a decision."

"You'd want to avoid temptation. Well, that's what I want, too! Precisely what I want! And in order to do it, I want to get that woman out of the way!"

Bob frowned and smiled a little as he did it. "You're really not suggesting that this hospital discharge a competent worker—just because—"

"I know it's extreme. But this thing requires extremities. Look!"

Colonel Ross sat down on the front edge of one of the deep chairs and leaned toward his audience. "Yesterday this —this woman came out to our place to ride. We did ride."

"Did you have to go along?" asked Garde.

"I—" Colonel Ross frowned. "No, but I did go. We rode. We came back, and—well, Libby stretched out on the grass —in the sun. She had on a yellow shirtwaist, or some such —a sweater, brown breeches. She had a little straw hat which she pushed forward over her face when she lay down. All you could see were her lips— her mouth—and, of course, the handsome, female length of her there on the grass—in the sun."

The doctors, listening, made their own pictures.

"Well," said the Colonel, "such a thing does get to a man! You know it does! Whatever he wants to happen—

"Then there's this. You know Mabel. She is not, and never was, the girl Libby Gillis is. Mabel could lie on the grass for hours at a time, and no man would quiver a muscle.

"But, just the same, I love Mabel! I have loved her. We've lived our lives together. Our sons were born, and tragedy took them from us. We've shared that—and other things. We came here to America, to breed and train and sell horses. We established our home here in Bayard. Now—I want to keep our life together. I want to—" For a minute he sat silent, his thoughts turning inward. Then he looked up at the two men who watched him. They were freely giving him their time; he was in trouble and needed help.

"I'm a *man*, too," the Colonel told them and himself. "With everything that means. Pride, physical hungers, or weakness, if you prefer. But above all that, I want to keep my home and my life as it now stands in the record book."

Bob Ruble stood up. "Then keep it!" he said sharply.

"You mean, I—" The Colonel looked up at him, startled, questioning.

"I mean all of us, I guess," said Bob. He walked over to the table and set his cup down.

"But don't come to us, sir," he said, with his back turned, "to have us take temptation from you. There are other attractive women in this town—and, I might remind you, other men who find Dr. Gillis attractive."

"You mean, maybe I'm not in as much danger as I think?"

"I'm no judge of that sort of risk."

"Mabel thinks she is."

Bob laughed and straightened the sleeve of his white gown. "I expect Bill Sims's wife is doing some judging, too," he suggested. "Not that I generally encourage gossip by passing the word along."

"It gets passed," the Colonel assured him morosely. "And you're quite right. Other men are after Libby—"

"Well, let's say, stirred by her. She's new—"

"She's damned handsome!"

"Yes, she is that."

"I've heard her name coupled with Willard Laurent's. I tried to tell Mabel that."

"Do any good?"

"No. She doesn't think Laurent would stand a chance against me." Now the Colonel was sheepish and almost ready to laugh at himself. "What about Windsor?" he asked. "There's smoke in that direction, too, isn't there?"

Dr. Ruble looked at his watch. Garde said he had a very sick child to check on.

Colonel Ross was not going to get any more conversation

from these men on the subject of Libby Gillis.

He drank his cold coffee. He picked up his straw hat and went out into the hospital corridor, along it to the front door. Behind him he was aware of a cart and people in green. He hurried his step. He'd try to stay out of Libby's way—if he could.

Chapter 8

THOSE DAYS EVERYONE WAS BEING ESPECIALLY NICE to Gene, and she had come to dread their tact and to hate it. She wanted things to be as they had been before Shawn had come to her home. She wished she could shut her eyes and dismiss, destroy this past month. She wanted the other wives to talk to her as they had always done.

But they did not. Just yesterday Ginny Ruble had said, "Oh, Gene, you're crazy!" Over some idea Gene had about letting her good cleaning woman go and hiring a crippled Negro woman from Fishtown.

But the minute the often-used phrase came out, Ginny had flushed and apologized—and before she had finished, she decided that she, too, might find some work for the unfortunates of the town. "But I won't give up Mag," she declared.

The other wives often thought Gene Cornel was "crazy" for the ideas she got. Maybe now they would never resume calling her that. Maybe now she would have to tell them more about her mother to make them understand—things.

When Ginny, partly to change the subject, had suggested the "old-fashioned Fourth of July picnic," Gene suspected that Ginny was doing the thing for her sake. She was not. She and the others were worried about Hazel, and Dewey. And this was not the wives' first effort to keep those two busy doing things together, things that would exclude Libby Gillis.

So that morning the wives gathered on the terrace beside the Ruble swimming pool and made their plans for the picnic. Hazel had not yet shown up, but they could start. They would, they decided, go at the matter as they did the Christmas and Thanksgiving dinners, which were big days with the four families.

"I use the summer to recover," said Nan plaintively.

"Just so you don't have a pageant," Ginny specified ruefully.

Gene and Nan laughed. This past week there had been a pageant, put on by the Girl Scouts, based magnificently upon the history of the Mississippi River. Eleven-year-old Jan Ruble had been a trapper, guiding her sled and dogs through the corn-flake snows.

"Ten dollars for a costume," groaned Ginny, "just to have her say 'mush!' "

Her friends were still laughing.

"Bob says he doubts if we should have fireworks," Ginny told them.

"But what is the Fourth without fireworks?" demanded Gene.

"He seems to think watermelon and potato salad will fill the gap."

"They won't."

"Of course they won't. And we'll have some fireworks. Pin wheels, Roman candles—the club does."

"Out on a pontoon boat in the middle of the river."

"Well—"

"Bob suggests we have our picnic supper, then go down to the club and watch their fireworks."

"Well—"

"I'm going to make homemade ice cream," Ginny planned. "And we'll have Hazel make a coconut cake."

"Oh, Ginny!"

"Her cakes are marvelous."

"But they take her two whole days, and we're all nervous wrecks . . ."

"But that's what we're aiming to do, isn't it?"

"To make—I said nervous wrecks, Ginny!"

"I know you did, Gene. But the object of things like this picnic—"

"Alison says he won't sit on the ground."

"Of course not. We'll have it right here."

"We could see the fireworks from the Sheltons'."

"They don't have room for a sack race."

"Good Heavens!"

"Have it at my house," said Gene. "We've room and can see the fireworks, too."

"All right, then. But Dewey is to cook the chicken. Nan, would you do the potato salad? Bob says he'll get watermelon."

"We'd better have a doctor on hand," drawled Gene. "Homemade ice cream, coconut cake, and watermelon."

Ginny laughed. "Well, maybe not watermelon."

"Be easier than the cake and ice cream . . ."

"I know, Gene, but—"

"Yes, yes. To keep Hazel busy—"

"And happy. With Dewey."

"Garde said," Nan offered, her eyes on her children who were playing with Sarah Ruble and the dogs, "that we should invite Dr. Gillis to our picnic. At least, he thinks we should ask her to some of our parties and gatherings."

"We don't invite any of the other hospital personnel," Ginny pointed out. Bob had been making the same sort of sounds.

"She's a doctor . . ."

"She also takes over," said Gene. "You know that she does."

"I said that to Garde, and he said it was our fault."

"Oh—men!"

"Anyway, why should we invite her? We do, to special things—like the luncheon Alison and Gene gave at the club for that big-shot doctor who spoke for Rotary. But our own affairs . . . She certainly can't be lonesome!"

"No, she isn't," said Gene. "And I doubt if she is ever apt to be."

"But haven't you noticed," said Ginny, her manner troubled, "that whenever we get together—oh, like at our table at the dinner dances, or when we were putting up the new awning on Nan's boat—the men have a way of bringing Libby into the group?"

"You mean, Dewey has a way."

"Well—"

"He does, Ginny! You might as well face it. Last Sunday, when we decided to put our noon meals together at Garde's, he stopped on his way home from church and asked Libby to come along."

"She didn't."

"No, but he asked her, and Hazel was just sick about it."

"I can't understand Dewey."

"I can!"

"Alison says Dewey feels responsible for her here—at least, at first."

"She's been here a month and, as has been said, she isn't lonely."

"Hazel says that Dewey's argument is that Libby enjoys our get-togethers."

"Did he say a thing like that?"

"Even Alison must think that was dumb!"

"Hush," warned Nan. "Hazel is coming—I saw her car through the bushes. We mustn't let her know what we are worrying about."

"I'm worried, all right," Ginny confessed. She and Nan both were checking on the children's whereabouts, with a car coming in.

Hazel joined the group in a flurry of explanations about

why she was late. The dog had got tangled in her stakeout leash—someone had phoned—"and I was setting the soaker and slipped. I sat down in a puddle and had to change my slacks!"

Everyone laughed. Ginny tried to tell her what they had planned for the picnic, though they really hadn't got far.

"I'm to blame," said Gene. "I asked Ginny if she was going to get Mary a black dress for college."

"The sorority girls seem to think it's a must," Ginny explained.

"Oh, sororities!"

"They're a part of college life, Gene."

"Maybe where Mary is going. My girl, remember, not only isn't as pretty as Mary, she didn't make the same college—"

This was a hypersensitive subject in the group. The girls had planned for years to go away together, and now Ginny must say again that she was sorry things had not worked out.

"I was disappointed," Gene agreed. "But Alison keeps telling me that Carol will be happier in the smaller school. It's quite good, and she probably could not have kept up with Mary at a big university. Of course, all of you tell me that I plan too much for the girls—"

"You do," said Ginny softly.

Gene's hands folded together tensely, about the sewing in her lap. "You would, too," she exclaimed. "I mean—perhaps if I told you about my mother ——"

Hazel sighed audibly, and both Nan and Ginny glanced at her, then at each other. Hazel was being relieved—she could show an interest in Gene's talk about her mother. It would draw everyone's attention away from her and her intimate concerns.

"You promised before to tell us," Hazel said quietly.

"Yes, I did. Well—" Gene picked up her sewing and began to set small stitches into the hem of the skirt. She could look at the green linen and not see the expressions on the faces of her friends. "My mother," she said, in a voice so soft it was difficult to hear, "was—is—Addie Burke. She is a concert pianist."

"Why, I've heard of her!" cried Ginny.

Briefly Gene looked at her.

"Of course you have," she said, so calmly that she sounded almost bored. "She's famous."

She stopped to thread her needle. "In fact," she continued, "She used to be *very* famous. She—"

She set the first stitch and a second. "She is—she was—a beautiful woman, as well." After a minute's hesitation she put down her sewing and looked earnestly at the others. Hazel, in the long chair, her shoes off, her gray slacks neatly creased, her white blouse snowy. Ginny in a blue-and-white checked dress, bare armed—little, cute Ginny. And pretty, dark-haired Nan in pink shorts and a pink-and-white-striped T shirt.

Then Gene looked at Hazel's shoes on the flagstones. "I mean, really beautiful," she said solemnly. "Her hair—it is red—and shining. Thick. Not like mine." Discontentedly, Gene's hand ruffled her troublesome locks. "She is a small woman—doll-like—but in spite of that, she has always had tremendous power in her wrists and hands. Of course she is talented, too. Very talented.

"And I didn't inherit any of it." Gene picked up her sewing again. "Looks—or talent. She made me learn to play the violin. She saw to it that I practiced, so I got fairly good at it."

"Yes, you are," said Ginny. Then she laughed, and the others joined in. They were remembering the time Gene had been persuaded to play for a Music Club program. She had practiced and practiced—and had played her first number beautifully. Then, during her second, a string had snapped. Muttering something about the weather and the damp strings, she had walked off the platform, leaving her audience sure, and shocked, that she had sworn at her violin.

Gene grinned. "I didn't want to play in the first place," she confessed. "In the very first place. But Addie made me. I hated it so. That was why I wouldn't buy a piano—or let the girls take lessons. Then I did let them."

"Carol is *good!*" said Ginny emphatically.

"Susan is, too," Gene pointed out, quickly defensive.

"Maybe their talent comes from their grandmother," said Nan, always ready to smooth out a troubled spot.

Gene smiled, a little wryly. "Any talent they have must come from her. But she is not a grandmother, Nan. In any sense of the word.

"And Susan is not like her. Nor Carol. I've tried hard, and I hope I have succeeded, in keeping them from being the selfish, self-centered girl my mother was raised to be." She glanced around at her friends.

"Look!" she said earnestly. "You are going to have to believe what I tell you about Addie, or there isn't any point in my talking about her!"

"We believe you, Gene," said Ginny, her face troubled. "It's just—"

"I know. I'd rather not believe she was what she was. But—I know her. And—"

"You don't have to tell us about her, if you don't want to," said Nan. "We love you as you are, and these things—your background—needn't matter."

Gene's eyes filled with tears. "I've been telling myself that for twenty years," she declared. "Then Shawn came here—" She gulped.

"How is he doing?"

"We won't hear anything for some weeks," said Gene. "And we were told not to write or go to see him. You know? I gave Alison fits for letting him come to our house—because of the girls and all—and go down to the beach with the rest of you. But Alison told me there was no danger; he was under drugs—"

"Tell us about your mother," said Hazel firmly. "Evidently you need to get a lot out of your system."

Gene nodded and sniffled. "I do," she sighed. "Well—where was I?"

"Selfish and self-centered," said Ginny helpfully.

"Oh, yes. Well—she was. You see, she was the daughter of great wealth. I mean—great. She was spoiled—indulged. But *that* backfired on *her* family—her selfishness, I mean—because she gave nine years of her youth to loving a worthless man. And no one could persuade her to do different. I guess she truly loved him. It's about the only sacrifice she ever made. But all the time she was studying, working, and beginning her career—though she was a prodigy at fourteen, and by the time she was twenty, she was famous—but all that time, and longer, she could see no man but this charming sot, the son of an 'old' family.

"I never saw him, of course, but Addie used to talk to us about him—to us kids, and to poor Mike."

"Who's Mike?" asked Ginny.

Gene looked surprised. "My father," she said as if anyone should know.

"But he wasn't . . . ?"

"He was not," Gene agreed. "No, this chap was a doctor —older than Addie, of course, but still young, and charming, and no good. Addie knew that he was no good, but she still clung to him. He got into troubles of various sorts, and finally he was arrested for some narcotic irregularity. Prescriptions sold, I've decided since I've come to know about such things. Anyway, he was arrested and then was too drunk to appear at the hearing.

"Because of all the publicity about it, this seemed to be the last straw, and Addie's parents, especially her younger brother, and the priest of the church, her business manager, too—all persuaded her that she simply could not go on planning to marry this man.

"But, on the way to keep a date with her—when she was

going to say these things to him—and while he was cold sober, he broke his leg."

"Oh, my!" said Nan.

"He would!" cried Ginny. They were enthralled with the story which Gene was telling.

"But that shouldn't have stopped her," said Hazel reasonably. "What's a broken leg?"

"A broken leg isn't much usually," Gene agreed. "And it wouldn't have stopped anything, perhaps, except that for this guy complications arose and caused a serious illness. The man really was in danger of dying—or, at least, losing his leg—and that was enough for Addie. She resumed their relationship."

"What sort of relationship was it?" asked Hazel.

"Oh, Addie was planning to marry him, some day. She was devoted to him—she came back to him after every tour or engagement—and he was devoted to her. I guess he was a leaky dreamboat, but he was hers. She knew that he sailed off in all the wrong directions, and she felt guilty about going back to him. She used to tell how she tried to cure herself of him."

"What did she do?" asked Ginny.

"She says she tried to stop being blind about him. She would compare him with every upright, likable man she knew so that he would show up for the heel he was. She tried to think of some unpleasant qualities he had. I guess how horrible he was when he was drunk. She insisted that she wanted to get to dislike him."

"But it didn't work," said Hazel.

"Oh, maybe it didn't work," Gene agreed. "More likely, she didn't really try those methods. I am pretty sure that is the way it was."

"But she *loved* the man!" cried Nan.

Gene smiled a little. "At any rate, she felt that she couldn't desert him—*fail him* was her term—now that he was crippled."

"Did she marry him?"

"No. But she and he—and his parents—went to a dozen places seeking a cure for him. I don't really know what it was—a bone infection, I suppose. Anyway, they went to every doctor in this country as well as to Switzerland, to England, and to Lourdes for the waters . . .

"And finally he was operated on and able to walk again. He also had stopped drinking."

"Oh, good!" sighed Nan.

"Did she marry him then?" asked Ginny excitedly.

Gene was folding her sewing. "I have to pick up the girls," she said. "I'll tell you, but it will have to be at another time."

"Gene . . ." said Ginny threateningly.

"I promise to tell you later," said Gene.

"You're going to tell us right now!"

"But—the girls—"

"They'll wait. You're never on time, anyway."

Which was true.

Gene looked at her watch; she jiggled from one foot to the other, then she sat down on the end of Hazel's chair.

"Well," she continued, "they went back home—the surgery had been done in Germany—and Addie resumed her career. Really, she was wonderful, you know. I have to say that, and you can read about it in any number of places. She was a small woman and exquisite. She knew exactly how to work herself up into a pitch of radiance and strength—this projected itself to her audiences. She knew exactly how to dress for a concert; she would come out on the stage—the lights just right on her red hair. She would have something glittery in it. She would be wearing a white dress, low on her shoulders, a full skirt, shining. She would sit at the piano, and play. She played beautifully. With great feeling, her touch as light as a cobweb, or rolling out in rich, full chords, brilliant cadenzas. And when she had finished, the people would stand and shout—it was all very wonderful. Flowers would be brought to her. . . . I have known people to say that once they had heard Addie Burke play Chopin or Liszt they needed never to hear those things played again. So far as her music went, I can say nothing bad about her. She was truly marvelous."

Gene was speaking in a thoughtful voice, her eyes down, her hands squeezing the roll of green linen which she held.

She was silent for a minute, then she sighed, heavily. "There was to be a three months' concert tour," she resumed, "and at the end of it she and this man whom she loved planned to be married. Addie was going to take a long vacation.

"The last concert of this final series was to be for the opening of a wonderful auditorium. Dr. Boussad was to join her there for that concert, then they were going to be married. Her family and her manager had become resigned to this and were hoping that things would work out.

"But—nothing worked out. Three days before the wedding Boussad went on a terrific bender. Addie was not told, because of the gala opening—nothing must upset her.

"The big night arrived. I know how it must have been backstage, the flowers, the telegrams, a few people allowed in to see her, to kiss her cheek; Addie screaming at her maid, whirling herself into a frenzy of excitement. In the auditorium music lovers and society people gathered for the opening of the hall. There were satins, perfumes, minks, and diamonds. The footlights went up, the velvet curtains parted, and Addie swept out upon the stage, the lighting skillfully manipulated to dramatize her low bow and changed subtly when she sat at the piano for her first number. It was a wonderful occasion. Addie was at the peak of her career, to have been selected to open this fine new hall . . .

"Then, at the end of her first group of numbers, when she was taking her bows, who should come roistering out upon the stage but Dr. Boussad, his clothes a mess. He was carrying a frazzled bouquet, and he was as drunk as a lord! It took a long minute to close the curtains—but in that minute he managed to disgrace Addie."

Gene sighed again.

"I guess the scene he made was pretty bad. Only Addie, the musician, could have gone on with the concert. In the papers the man was identified as only 'an overexuberant fan.'

"But however bad was the scene he made onstage, it must have paled before the one the next day, when Addie told Boussad she was *through*. Even when she used to tell us about it, her eyes would flash, and she would pace up and down the room. She had, in her travels and studies, acquired all sorts of mannerisms, you know. And she would put in French words, German and Italian ones—well, anyway, when Addie was excited, you knew it.

"I imagine she put on the performance of her life for Dr. Boussad. She said, afterward, that she hoped perhaps to shock him into a recognition of what he had done and into changing his behavior. Of course, she told him that she did not love him, that she could not marry him, and that she never wanted to see him again.

"She didn't expect to be taken literally. But—he did believe her. He left her and he killed himself."

"Oh, no!" gasped Nan. Ginny looked ready to cry. Hazel sat up on the chaise and put on her shoes.

"He had to," she decided.

"Well, anyway—he did," said Gene. "He went down to the beach, walked out into the ocean—and drowned."

She stood and smoothed her bundle of linen.

The three women watched her and waited. "There must be more . . ." said Ginny anxiously.

"There is," said Gene. She looked tired.

"You'll tell us, won't you?"

"Ye-es. I suppose I'll have to tell you."

"We'll see that you do."

"All right. But not now. Now I have to take Carol to the dentist, and—well—" She walked away from them, over to the station wagon.

Her friends watched her, watched her drive away.

"Gene's a real person," said Hazel thoughtfully.

"Oh, she is!" agreed Ginny. "Honest as they come—blunt and frank, but always dependably honest."

They all thought about Gene, in her gingham dress, saying the things she had said. "She's nice . . ." murmured Ginny.

"And scared to death," Hazel decided.

"Why?" asked Ginny. "These things she is telling about are all in the past . . ."

"For heaven's sake, Ginny! She's telling them because of her brother and his—his illness."

"Oh," said Ginny. Then she frowned and looked up. "You mean—she's scared about Carol?" she asked, almost whispering.

"That's what she is scared about."

"But Carol isn't—" cried Nan. "Oh, I maybe shouldn't say this, but the doctor—the psychiatrist—doesn't think Shawn's trouble is an inherited thing."

"That's true," agreed Hazel. "He traces it to trauma—environment—his childhood pressures and demands. And he—the psychiatrist—he told Gene that if Shawn's childhood was such that it would explain his present condition—"

"She needn't worry about Carol!" concluded Ginny triumphantly.

"But she *is* worrying. Doesn't she believe this doctor?"

"I think she is trying to believe him, Hazel. I think that is why she is going back over the past, to argue that the situation was such as to explain—to argue with herself, I mean."

Chapter 9

FOURTH OF JULY CAME, WITH A BLAZING SUN. "What did you expect?" Alison asked his wife, when she began to wilt over the preparations for their picnic. The flag must be out, the picnic tables set up on the terrace . . .

"I'm glad we cut it down just to the afternoon and evening," Gene panted.

"So am I," said Alison, preparing to go off to the hospital. He wanted to check on the Ewers child who had just barely survived the delayed surgery and was making a slow recovery.

"You come back at noon!" said Gene strongly.

"I shall. Though under emergency conditions—shooting, drowning, sunstroke—"

"Who's on call?"

"Windsor."

"All right. But everyone is coming at three, and there are things you can do."

"I'll bet I do them, too," her husband told himself.

The picnic was fun, really. The small children had a fine time with pink lemonade and ice cream cones, popcorn, and little flags to wave. The teen-agers played records and danced on the porch—and tried to be bored with sack races and other puerile efforts thought up by their parents.

"Who's going to make the speech?" Dewey kept asking, until, at five o'clock, he was called to the hospital.

Someone else would have to cook the chicken—someone else did. And ate it, too. Because Dewey did not return until it was dark that evening and Nan had already taken her little ones home. Sarah Ruble was sleeping on the couch in the Cornel den, and everyone else was limp.

"Where in the world have you been?" Hazel demanded of her husband.

The other doctors looked at Windsor with great interest. If he had had enough in the way of emergencies to keep him busy at the hospital for four hours, they were asking, why hadn't he sent for another doctor?

"Are you hungry?" Gene asked him.

Dewey stretched his arms high over his head. "No, I ate

at the hospital. They had flags on their ice-cream cups, too."

"What called you?" asked Bob. "It must have been *some-thing!*"

"It was enough," Dewey agreed. He sat down on the swing. "Is all the work done around here?"

"You timed it just fine," Garde assured him.

"I hoped to. Well, I knew what I was being called for. Even if I hadn't been the one on call, I would have gone for that case. It was uremia, and I was pretty sure the woman would arrive in a dying condition.

"But it turned out there were some complications. First, I had to wait around for over an hour, then we learned that the ambulance bringing the case in had been in a crash with a car running a red light. When it finally did come in—the case, I mean—the woman had a rather bad cut on her face, but that was not the cause of death."

"Can you prove that?" Alison asked him.

"Can you prove it was?"

"I didn't see the case. But the family might want to prove that the wreck was—"

"How soon did she die after coming in?" asked Garde.

"Half an hour. And it was uremia that killed her. The death certificate says so."

"I hope you had the sense to order an autopsy," said Dr. Cornel.

Dewey stood up. "The family wouldn't consent. So that leaves me with just enough sense now to go home to bed. Are you ready, Hazel?"

"I'm ready—but I have my own car. It's loaded."

"Was he mad?" asked Ginny, when she and Bob departed.

"Who?"

"Dewey."

"Huffy. He'll get over it. Sooner than he will over Hazel's questions."

"What sort of questions?"

"She'll ask some. All the time he was talking she was

doing arithmetic. Dewey was at the hospital for a good two hours longer than that case explains. And she is going to ask him about those two hours. These days she is watching Dewey like a hawk."

Hazel was; she had done her arithmetic—and she did ask Dewey to account for all the time he had been away from the picnic.

The next morning his friends, the doctors, asked him the same things, and he gave them the same answers. "About seven I ate supper, and I got to talking to Libby."

"Libby?"

"She'd been at the club. A youngster burned his hand on a sparkler. Libby brought him to the hospital for a tetanus shot. After that—we got to talking."

"What about?" asked Bob Ruble. The men had gathered for a staff meeting, which they hoped to keep short. The uremia case, and death, had been an item. They could smell a law suit against the driver of the car which had collided with the ambulance, and they wanted the hospital records in order.

"Oh," said Dewey, "we talked about fireworks and how they always shot them off too early. And then we talked about socialized medicine . . ."

"I'll bet," said Dr. Cornel.

"We did!"

Libby in a pale-blue blouse and dark-blue shorts, sandals sugar-white at the end of her long, satiny brown legs . . . Hazel had not believed the socialized-medicine bit either.

"Something brought it up," said Dewey. "I don't know what it was. And she asked if our clinic was not, really, social medicine in practice. And I told her it wasn't—that we were four doctors working together as individuals in a single hospital, that we had staff conferences, and a tissue committee, things like that—but we were certainly not under the administration of the government or the state. Nor was there any compulsion on the patient—"

"And you spent two whole hours talking about that sort of thing?" Bob asked in wide-eyed wonder.

Dewey looked angry. "I have patients waiting . . ." he reminded the others. "This meeting was called about a uremia case, I believe."

"And we have discussed it," Dr. Cornel reminded him. "You write that thing up damn carefully, will you, Windsor? Make a careful chart of the face injuries—"

"Yes, sir," said Dewey, his face still red.

"And watch your spelling while you're at it," Cornel continued. "In fact, I think we can all be reminded to write more clearly, and spell more exactly, in our reports and certainly in our orders."

"What's happened now?" asked Garde apprehensively.

"Mrs. Dyer is as mad as hops," Alison said, "about being forced to go through a BMR this morning."

Dewey's head snapped up. "I didn't order any BMR for her!" he cried.

"I know you didn't," said Alison. "But the nurse read your orders as BMR—and they rather forcibly made Mrs. Dyer—"

"She says she won't pay for it!" Bob laughed. "She is really mad, Windsor."

"I'll go see what happened—"

"Sit still," Dr. Cornel told him. "We have already figured out what happened. You admitted her yesterday morning and wrote on her chart that she was to have 'BPR.'"

"Bathroom privileges!" said Dewey loudly.

"Of course. But the nurse read it BMR, and the test was made."

"The dumb—" groaned Dewey.

"The poor handwriting," the Chief of Staff amended. The other two men were laughing.

"We all have to be more careful," Dr. Cornel pointed out. "We all have had experience with confused orders. We get in a hurry . . . If Windsor had written his order out, or told his patient what he had written— Fortunately no harm was done." He paused, then he looked sternly at his colleague. "I hope the same can be said about last night, Dewey."

"Now, what do you mean by that?"

"Oh, your leaving the picnic early—your staying away for four hours. What in *thunder* did you tell Hazel?"

"The same as I told you." Dewey got up, walked to the window, and stood looking out at the parking lot, anger in every line of his back.

"That you had a case," said the Chief of Staff calmly, "that you got to talking to Libby Gillis, that you lost all track of time . . ."

Dewey said nothing.

"How did she take it?" Bob asked, his face concerned.

Dewey whirled about; his checks were scarlet, and his blue eyes were blazing. "What was there to *take?*" he demanded. "I told her exactly what happened!"

"For Pete's sake, Dewey!" cried Bob. The other men echoed him. Dewey should be more thoughtful, they said. He should not do things that confirmed Hazel's ideas about him and Libby. Didn't he have a lick of sense?

Each thing they said intensified Dewey's anger. Finally he strode to the door, turned, and faced his friends. "What is this, anyway?" he cried. "Why should I be put on the carpet this way? You don't like my handling of a case! You don't like the way I write my orders! You don't like the way I talk to my wife! Well, do you know how matters look to me? I think that you guys are presuming on our association, and, quite frankly, I don't like *that* situation!"

He opened the door and, heels pounding, he strode out into the hall.

The men left behind looked gravely at each other.

"He said he would harelip the whole clinic," Alison reminded the others. "It does begin to look as if he were going to do it."

"We can't let him!" cried Garde.

"Can we stop him?" asked the Chief of Staff.

Only three days after the picnic the word went around among the wives that Hazel was giving a dinner party. None of the other three wives was invited, but they felt pretty sure that Hazel could use their help.

Ginny Ruble cut a bowl full of nasturtiums, put small Sarah into her older sister Mary's care, gave Bobby and Jan their orders, and then she drove over to the Windsors'. Nan was coming down the street from the other direction.

"I thought I could maybe run some errands for Hazel," she explained as she and Ginny went through the garage. Gene was already in the house, looking critically at the table which Hazel was setting.

"Hi, girls," she said. "Hazel's giving a party."

"We heard. Who's coming?" Ginny carried her bowl of nasturtiums into the living room.

"Oh, the bunch we sometimes play bridge with," said Hazel, rubbing her hand back over her hair.

There was such a "bunch." Four couples—with no fixed time for a dinner and bridge session. Gene and Alison usually played with the group.

"Tonight," said Hazel, in answer to the unspoken reminder, "Willard Laurent is coming with Libby Gillis."

A little icicle of silence formed in the dining room.

"Whose idea was that?" asked Gene. Of course, it did explain why she and Alison had not been invited.

"Well—Dewey thinks we should do things for Libby," said Hazel distractedly. "And Willard is a single man—he's shown interest in Libby."

"Are you playing Cupid?" asked Ginny, as forthrightly as her daughter Jan might have done.

"No—well, don't you think she should be paired with single men?" asked Hazel.

"What are you feeding them?" Ginny asked, wandering toward the kitchen. She was not going to encourage much talk about Libby.

They never got anywhere on that subject. By then the wives' opinion on Libby was fixed. She had style, she was clever—and they thought Dewey was making a fool of himself to push her into everything that went on in town. Libby herself had no interest in the activities of the wives—and the families—that made up the hospital group. Her idea of *nothing* was a gathering where the wives and children cluttered the scene. They—

Ginny lifted a pan lid, then she opened the refrigerator door.

"I'm having a standing rib," said Hazel hastily. "I thought—"

"Roast beef in July?" cried Nan.

"We're air-conditioned."

"Yes, you are, but—"

"I'm not making gravy and stuff," Hazel defended her menu. "Then—I thought I would fix sweet potatoes with orange sauce the way Ginny does . . ."

"Not with roast beef, Hazel," Ginny protested gently. "They don't go."

"Why not? And I don't want to make gravy. So I am having sweet potatoes and asparagus—and yellow lima beans, with pimento added to them for color." Distraught, she looked around at her friends for encouragement.

"What dessert?" asked Gene hardily.

"Well, I've made a lemon cake—I got up early and baked it, and I'll ice it right after lunch. I thought I'd serve it with ice-cream bars."

"*Hazel!*" The protest came in a single blast.

"Why not?" she asked, looking ready to cry. "Those bars are good. I'll unwrap them, and they'll look all right on the plate with a slice of cake—and anyway—anyway—" Now she was crying, and she did not do it prettily.

"Whatever I do," she sobbed, "it will be a mess."

"It doesn't need to be," Gene assured her.

"That's right," Ginny added. "Now, look—if you've already bought the roast, you're to make mashed potatoes and gravy. And you're not going to serve ice-cream bars. Of all things!"

Hazel dropped to a chair and buried her head in her arms; she was weeping uncontrollably. "No one," she sobbed, "no one likes the things I do—these days."

Ginny brought Cokes from the refrigerator. Gene urged Hazel to her feet and led her out to the breezeway.

"They don't like what you are doing," said Ginny, "because you are not doing what you can these days, Hazel."

"I'm not?" Hazel wiped her cheeks with the tissue which Nan brought her.

"Of course you're not. To serve yellow lima beans in midsummer! And no salad. Hazel, you aren't *trying!*"

"Well, what should I do?"

"We'll help you."

They did. The menu was revised—built around the roast, which was on hand, but the potatoes should be a soufflé and gravy provided. The lima beans must be fresh ones—Gene would drive out to Stelljes' for some—and if there were fresh pineapples available, Hazel's salad could be diced fruit put into the hollowed-out halves. "Keep the leaves on. They look fresh and cool." She could put red raspberries on the lemon cake, with whipped cream available but not put on.

The wives worked until eleven-thirty and then sat down again in the breezeway before they would need to gather their families together for twelve-thirty lunch.

Hazel was looking better—more calm, and more able to cope with the evening's party. Gene promised to come back after three and check on things. Meanwhile everyone was busily shelling the lima beans.

"Gene," suggested Ginny Ruble, "why don't you give us the second installment of your story about your mother's romance?" There was a firmness in her voice.

Gene's head snapped up, but Ginny's blue eyes were firm, too.

"All right," sighed Gene. "I guess I can. Let's see—where did I leave off?"

Three voices told her.

"The doctor had walked into the ocean."

"The man she loved killed himself."

"She must have got over it enough to marry your father."

Gene nodded. "She did. Marry him, I mean. I don't know whether Addie ever got over Dr. Boussad. But—anyway, within six months after his death, she married Mike Burke. He was—he was her brother's roommate at college. A rising football star—and he was thirteen years younger than Addie. He was twenty." Gene shredded the bean pod in her hands. "He was," she continued, her voice drained of all emotion, "he was a tall man. Very tall. And thin as the years went by. Most men get fat. Mike got thin. He was not really handsome. His face was rather like that of a good-looking horse. Long, you know. His nose was large, and he had deep creases in his cheeks, which one had better not call dimples. His voice was deep, and there was a sort of elegance about him— the way he dressed, and did—"

"You loved him," said Nan softly.

Gene looked up at her. "Everyone loved Mike," she said softly.

"But how—" asked Hazel. "How did your mother ever marry such a man—younger, and evidently popular?"

Gene shook her head a little and picked up a fresh handful of beans.

"It wasn't hard—for Addie, I guess. Remember, she was a very glamorous woman—and beautiful. She really was beautiful. She was renowned—people made a fuss over her. It was as if a spotlight was always upon her. And—well, it must have been as if—well—as if someone like Elizabeth Taylor, or Eydie Gormé—someone like that today—should suddenly decide to make a play for Bobby Ruble."

"Oh, my," said Bobby's mother.

"Yes!" Gene agreed. "My mother had all that glamour, and more. Women did, those days. Garbo, Joan Crawford —and Addie Burke. She had traveled the world; she knew everybody; she was beautiful—vivacious. Small, redhaired, with lovely eyes that sparkled like jewels. Besides, for her own purposes, when she wanted something, Addie could act the woman she looked instead of the woman she was. She could *be* fragile and helpless—and I've seen that act, often, bolster some man's ego. As I suppose it bolstered Mike's. Remember, he was only twenty.

"Anyway, she married him and, still bolstering, she changed her name, mid-career. I imagine her agents made a fuss. Because she often told pridefully that she had got away with doing such a thing. One had to be, she told, really good —her career really and firmly established—to do such a thing and get away with it. Addie was never exactly the modest type."

Ginny brushed the scattered bean pods into a pile. "I've been thinking of Bobby," she mused. "Of course, he's only sixteen and—well— But why would a woman of thirty-three, rich, famous, beautiful—I can't see Libby Gillis falling for Bobby."

The women laughed merrily.

"She's not rich," Hazel pointed out.

"Oh, well, that isn't the point. But why did Gene's mother —this Addie she tells about—why did she *want* to marry a college sophomore?"

They all looked at Gene.

"Was there some reason?" Hazel asked. "I mean, a definite one?"

"Yes," Gene said slowly. "I've thought about that, too. And I'm pretty sure I have the answer. Knowing my mother, how spoiled she was—she literally could not endure being thwarted! And then one must remember that she had given nine years of her life to Dr. Boussad. She really loved him, but she had never known his love, lived with him, I mean. His death cut off any chance of expressing her passion. She had been the one to put off their marriage, but when, suddenly, the door was closed upon *that*—well, Addie looked about for a young and virile man. Mike was in her line of sight, and she went after him, married him, and she had three babies within the first four years of that marriage."

Hazel snorted.

Ginny laughed.

"Were you one of them?" Nan asked.

"I was," said Gene. "I was the youngest. There were three of us girls."

"Oh, that must have been fun!" said Ginny.

"It was not!" Gene looked grim and sounded grim. She gazed beyond her friends, out through the screen to the street. . . . A convertible went past, three boys in T shirts, two girls with flying head scarves. The laundry delivery truck came into view, and a scooter, a black sedan . . .

"Our family, our home," said Gene tightly, "was never notable for its fun. You see—" She paused again, and the others waited.

"You see," she tried again, after taking a deep breath. "I—well—there was this: Mike wanted to work. I believe right from the first he wanted to work and to be his own man. I know, when I was still a little girl, he would get jobs. Once he was a coach at a high school. But Addie always insisted that he travel with her, on her tours. They quarreled about it. They quarreled about a lot of things—sometimes terribly. I remember how frightened I used to be at the way they looked, the way they shouted. Sometimes I find myself yelling at my girls, and then I'll hear Addie's voice in mine, and I am ashamed.

"But Mike—I suppose he realized quite soon that things were not right. The difference in their ages and interest, Addie earning the money for the family and home. But there wasn't much he could do or did do. The laws of his church—

and hers, too, of course—did not countenance divorce."

Gene traced her finger tip down the line separating the columns of the newspaper spread upon the table. "It is odd," she said wryly. "I can see now how odd it was that the only strength his church, and Addie's, ever exerted in our family, on our home, was the matter of marriage and divorce. It need not have been that way. I've learned that much about the church.

"It would not have countenanced a home based on hatred —and passion.

"We children—we grew up knowing lavish gifts and abandonment to servants, to school, to camps. Sometimes there was affection—Mike loved us, I am sure. And Addie would sweep down on us with gifts. I had a fur coat when I was eight. Gray squirrel, with a cap to match. But we knew neglect, too. Real neglect. My hair would not be cut or washed. And often I had no stockings to wear. Literally none!

"We would be brought home, or we would be taken to some vacation spot, and then become the victims of our parents' boredom, their impatience with us—and with life, too, I suppose.

"Mike could be, and was, vindictive toward Addie. Then he would be thoroughly ashamed of himself and try to make up. Those times never lasted. He hated Addie's long hours of practice. It does get to you, you know. Hour after hour of scales, hour after hour of working on a single cadenza, the whole house shaking with the pounding noise of it.

"Mike hated Addie's friends—the other artists, the impresarios, the hangers-on, the gushing, the posturing—and he would think up ways to thwart Addie or humiliate her. He would do little mean things like changing their hotel reservations from a big, plush hotel to some awful one down in the dumps, or he would deliberately leave behind a piece of luggage with her jewels or even her gowns. Maybe he would 'lose' just one of her shoes.

"They quarreled bitterly over such things. They quarreled—and then made up in passionate reunions that were worse than the quarrels. I could—I could go into this in great detail. I won't. But we children soon had ways of gauging the family peace. 'Mother is on tour' meant that we could join the Camp Fire girls and have cook-outs in our garden. 'Mother is at home, resting,' meant that we had better make ourselves scarce, go to the movies, and hang around the shopping centers of whatever suburb we then graced with our domicile.

" 'Mother is at home—working—practicing . . .' She practiced at night; she practiced six hours a day, and meals were served at all hours. One couldn't keep servants. And Mike . . .

"Of course she had to practice, and even when we had, for weeks, listened to her readying a concert, those times that we were taken to hear her—and see her—goose pimples would bump up on our arms, and we stood up with the others and yelled 'Brava' and 'Bis' with the best of them."

" 'Bis'?" asked Ginny.

"That means again, or encore. I think it does. Anyway, we said it.

"But we hated the heavy practice sessions, too. Under the noise of her playing, we kids got away with murder. The servants wouldn't stay. Addie would be playing or sleeping. Mike was off on his own sorts of business. And we kids did every crazy thing in the book, not so much because we *wanted* to do them—there just wasn't anyone to say 'No.'

"The practicing was bad, but the concert season could be bad, too. If there should be an unfavorable review, we all were in for a very difficult time. Addie didn't get many bad notices, but of course she occasionally did, and those reviews devastated her.

"I remember one time—I memorized that review, because there was so much fuss. I think I can still quote from it.

118

"Addie, you see, was to play Rachmaninoff's *C Minor Concerto* with a symphony orchestra. This was in Philadelphia. By then we had bought the New York town house. She came home and got the reviews the morning—the noon —after the concert. Her manager brought the papers to the house, and, well, it was—something." Gene's voice sloughed away tiredly.

"Tell us," said Ginny. It was getting late, but no one wanted to leave.

Gene nodded and rested her head on her hand. "As I say, I still remember it. This particular reviewer—Addie valued his opinion. And I suppose the music world did. Anyway, he wrote, 'Miss Burke suffered a stroke of bad luck during the first movement in the form of a memory lapse.' "

"Oh . . ." sighed Ginny.

Gene glanced at her. "Yes. And Addie must have known that such a thing was bad. Maybe she hoped the reviewer would not mention it. But he did. He went on to tell that proceedings were suspended for a few seconds while she took a quick look at the score, then things went on, he said, as intended. His review went on, too. He said, 'Miss Burke's formulation of phrase and line indicated a superior order of musicianship, but this general qualification apparently was not enough to make this particular composition sound with conviction. In Rachmaninoff's larger works the heaving heart beat is all important, and any attempt to moderate his special character in the light of a more fastidious conception is likely to make it seem tentative. It wasn't loud enough, nor plushy enough.' "

"Oh, dear," said Ginny.

"You did memorize it," said Nan admiringly.

"You would, too, if you had heard nothing else for hours and hours and hours. Addie put on a scene which lasted for days. She read the thing—she quoted it. She screamed, she sobbed. This went on and on, and finally Mike took her in his arms to comfort her. She clung to him—and—well, it got pretty darn passionate there in our living room. We girls just sat and stared, and Mike caught one of us doing it, and he yelled at us to '*Get out!*' which we did, feeling very odd, especially because we could hear Mike, in the room we had left, cursing Addie."

Gene sighed. "Well, that's the way my childhood home was, and—whatever was going on, wherever we lived—there was never any peace. We kids didn't have one thing which we could count on. We knew no security of any sort.

"They—our parents—did everything for us. Schools, camps, fur coats, spending money. And at the same time they did nothing for us. Literally nothing. I never remember my mother washing my face or binding up a cut finger or—or—

"She quarreled constantly with Mike, and she carried her quarrel over to her relationship with her children. She 'adored' us—this usually in public. I remember once when she bought us girls quaint nightgowns and had our long, lank hair tied back with *Alice in Wonderland* ribbons, and she rehearsed us to come down and say good night before guests at some dinner party. She knew and played her part, too.

"She brought us extravagant gifts from her travels—everything from a Sicilian donkey and cart to jeweled music boxes.

"She could be extremely ugly to us as well. Pointing out that my hair was thin and my face plain—hurting us, because she was hurt by something Mike had said or done.

"Mike—he would play with us wildly. I remember a playhouse he built for us and helped us furnish. He would even share the tea parties we would have. And that was wonderful—except that the next week he would walk past us as if we did not exist, not answering if we spoke to him.

"And once—once—" Gene sat thoughtful, her face drawn and pale. "Once," she said, lifting her head, "he told us that he hated us, that we tied him to Addie and her accursed piano—and he hated us. I don't think I'll ever forget that. He was so deadly cold and earnest, so—so—"

Ginny reached for her hand. Nan and Hazel were not able to look at Gene. They wished they had not asked her to tell more about her family. Sometimes they had glimpsed a shadow of this same sort of anger, this frenzy of frustration, in Gene. If the girls did not do well in school, if Carol was silly, or Susan clumsy, Gene went all to pieces. It took Alison to calm her. . . .

"We," said Gene, resuming again, "acquired quite early an ugly education in sex through the quarrels and reconciliations of our parents. I remember—

"Shawn was born when I was ten. Addie was whimsical —and wry—about it. She made jokes to her friends. Mike —Mike was angry. And during that year we learned that love was shameful trickery and marriage a state of binding slavery. It—it was hard for me to believe that it could be—anything else."

"Well, you do believe it now," said Ginny briskly.

Nan stood up. "You mustn't tell any more," she said firmly. "You were right to put all this behind you and build for yourself a life that is good and true."

"That's right," Ginny agreed. Hazel echoed her.

Gene sat smiling, her face wistful.

Ginny gathered up the bean pods. Nan put cold water on the beans and told Hazel how to cook them. "I have to run . . ." she said then.

"So do I," said Ginny, watching Gene from the corner of her eye. She was all right—she would be. Now she stood up slowly and smoothed her skirt.

"Hazel," she said, turning to her friend, "you be careful of what you wear tonight."

"Well, I thought—"

"Wear that silk print jacket and skirt, with the little white blouse. It's wonderful on you."

"Lena's coming to serve, isn't she?" Ginny added her bit. "So—yes, you wear that dress. Gene is right. It is good on you. And these days you want to look and do and be as good as you can, Hazel."

Hazel nodded. "I want to be . . ." she agreed.

"Then you can be. If you work at it."

Chapter 10

A DAY COULD START, THE DOCTORS WERE TO mention later, and go along, seeming monotonous in its regularity. Then, with the hospital halls clear and shining, the nurses going quietly about their duties, the patients drowsing in their rooms, a bell could ring, and a second one. The emergency room would come alive—basins would be uncovered, lights turned on—and suddenly nothing would be routine or at all monotonous.

That day in mid-July was such a time. The morning had gone so quietly that all the doctors could talk about when they gathered for lunch was the man from the city who had come to their decent little town, checked in at the rather fusty old hotel, and gone on a monumental drunk.

"His clothes were good," said Dr. Windsor who, the afternoon before, had been called by the hotel manager, in hopes that the doctor would pronounce the man sick and so get him out of the place by ambulance. "But the smell of that room when I walked in—*geek!*"

"He wasn't sick," said Alison dryly.

Dewey shrugged. "Any man at the end of a four-day bender . . . Look! There were a half-dozen empty whisky bottles—fifths. He had, sometime during the session, sent for food. There was evidence of an old hamburger and a stained coffee cup. The carpet was literally thick with ciga-rette stubs. You know how some men crease and bend their stubs. So the place looked to be crawling with grub worms. And this man—on the bed—half dressed—sure he was sick! But he didn't belong in our hospital."

"What did you do?"

"I told the manager to locate his family and get the police to help them. Naturally the hotel people want him out of there. But unless he gets disorderly, or doesn't pay his bill—"

"That's the law?"

Dewey shrugged. "I think it probably is the law."

"What will happen to him?" asked Libby. "If neither his family or the police are sent for?"

"He's drunk up his liquor," said Dewey. "At least, there was no full bottle in evidence. He'll sleep for a day, perhaps, spend another feeling awful, then he will shave and go home, looking like the tail of a dog caught in a swamp, and—"

"Have to think up something to tell his wife." Libby laughed.

"He'll tell her something, and she won't believe it," Bob decided. "This chicken is good! I'll tell the kitchen."

"The only time," said Alison Cornel, "that we have chicken here in the middle of the week is when Gene is planning to have it for dinner."

"How do you know she plans to have . . . ?"

"She told me. The preacher is coming for dinner, and she is going to have chicken. That's the law, too."

"Why is the preacher coming?" asked Libby casually.

"Why?" Dr. Cornel considered her question. "I don't believe there is any special reason. We just entertain the rector now and then."

"Are you prepared to entertain him?" asked Dewey. Dr. Cornel should have recognized his tone and manner and been warned.

But, "Gene's cooking chicken," said Alison good-naturedly. He reached for a roll.

123

"Oh, but you'll have to talk to him," Dewey pointed out. Bob and Garde exchanged glances, their eyes twinkling.

"I don't often find myself at a loss for words," Cornel reminded Dewey.

"But Welch is a *preacher,* man!" Dewey pointed out earnestly. "You can't talk to him about your mulch pile or why the ivy doesn't grow on the southeast corner of your house . . ."

"I think I've got it started this year," said Alison eagerly.

"Will Mr. Welch be interested?" Dewey asked intently.

"No. Maybe not. He—I don't think he is a yard-and-garden man."

"He isn't much of any kind of man except a preacher," Dewey agreed.

"He's interested in social matters. I can talk about the school board, and—" Now Dr. Cornel was beginning to look bothered.

"Yes. That's a subject which interests you."

"Hey, look," said Alison, "are you needling me?"

"Oh, I wouldn't!" cried Dewey innocently. "But I have a longer history of dinners for the preacher than you have, my boy. Up to this last year you weren't exposed to such things. So my advice is: have a topic—a gambit—something to get the talk going."

Alison poured cream on his peach pie. "As for instance?" he growled.

"Well—oh, you could discuss the differences between Pentacostal and Evangelical churches."

"Not me. I don't know the differences."

"You could look it up. Or you could ask him if you were right in your knowledge of the differences between an atheist, an agnostic, and an infidel. Do you know *those* differences?"

"I think so."

"Or you could look those words up, too."

"I don't need to look them up!" said Dr. Cornel, getting red.

"Well, maybe not," Dewey agreed, his tone bland. "That way you probably can start off the evening with a mild, and I hope polite, argument with Father Welch."

"Look here, Windsor!" shouted the goaded Dr. Cornel. "What makes you think I'm not smart enough to know the correct meaning of such words?"

Dewey shrugged. "I was only trying to help."

"You were *not* trying to help! For all I know you'd talk me into using your silly device, and then it would develop that you had used the same thing the last time Welch came to your house!"

Garde and Bob both laughed. But Dewey shook his head. "I wouldn't do such a thing, Cornel," he protested.

"I am not at all sure of what you would do, Windsor, to work out what you consider a joke."

At this point Dewey might have laughed and shrugged. The others might have laughed, too. Laughing, Cornel might have risen to look up the words in the dictionary. This sort of development was common in the group.

But—that day—Dewey got mad. Unexpectedly, and without justification, it seemed.

He stood up abruptly. He said, with icy dignity, that he had indeed tried to be helpful and that, in addition, he was damn sick and tired of being considered the clown of the organization.

"I didn't say—" Alison attempted.

Garde and Bob looked at each other. Was Dewey still setting up an act?

"I know damn well what you said," cried Dewey. "And if it's all the same to you, Cornel, I will ask you *not* to say such things to me again. I can be, and am, as serious a doctor as any of you. I was entirely serious in wanting you to present yourself well with Father Welch—"

"What's wrong with me acting myself?" Dr. Cornel demanded, his own choler up.

"Try it and find out," said Dewey, preparing to leave.

"Hey!" cried Bob. "Dewey! You can't go away mad. Cornel . . . ?"

"Let him go," growled the chief. "I've nothing more to say to him."

Dewey slammed the door.

"He *was* mad," said Garde, as if he couldn't believe it.

"So what?" asked Libby. "We all get mad now and then." She didn't understand. And no one was about to explain things to her.

"If you don't think I'll be needed," she said to Dr. Cornel, after an uneasy minute, "I think I'll go on home."

He lifted his hand and nodded. He was angry himself. Not at any of the fool things which Windsor had said, but— well, the whole ridiculous scene . . .

It was right then that the first bell rang.

And then the second one . . .

"Try to hold Gillis until we see how bad this accident is," said Dr. Cornel, walking fast toward the emergency room.

He got the first case, brought out of the first ambulance. Bob Ruble and Garde Shelton took the second one to o.r. It was the worst one, and Cornel should have been the one on it.

It was all one accident, which had involved three vehicles, but only two of the drivers were injured. Mrs. White, Cornel's case, not too badly—cuts and shock . . .

While the other . . .

"It's the worst impact case I have ever seen!" Alison declared when, three hours later, he was cleaning up. "And I have seen a few airplane crash victims, too. But this man— his skull, both arms, his hip, knees, ankles . . . When I went into o.r., Shelton showed me a section of his leg bone which just fell out when he and Bob were examining the poor guy."

"Will he live?" asked the reporter who had been waiting for this answer.

Dr. Cornel shook his head. "I don't know why he is alive now. What happened? Do you know?"

"Yes. Some of it. There was this truck following Mc-Clung's car, you know. He said it looked to him as if Mc-Clung had veered across the line and clipped the fender of the White water truck. It was empty. He just seemed to drive right at that truck. After hitting it, this man said—the third driver, you know—McClung's car just rose up into the air, and the rear of it crashed into *him*—into the windshield and vent of the large truck following.

"After that crash, McClung's automobile came to a rest in the middle of the highway. The following truck wasn't too badly damaged—it could be driven out of the way, and the driver of it wasn't hurt at all.

"Mrs. White's water truck lost its front wheel and axle, slid across the road and into a ditch; the tank was torn off. Is she hurt?"

Dr. Cornel shook his head. "She wasn't thrown out. But McClung . . ."

The reporter winced. "Yeah, man! He was knocked out of the left front door—the truck driver said he just sat helpless and watched the whole thing—but McClung's leg caught, and his head and shoulders struck the pavement before the car came to a stop. His car was completely demolished, Doctor—and the man must have lost quarts of blood!"

"He did," said the surgeon wearily.

"How bad . . . ?"

"Oh, at this point we can only guess. We took x-rays, but they'll all have to be done over. The man is unconscious. He has severe head injuries, compound fracture of the left thigh, compound fracture of the right knee, fracture and dislocation of the left ankle, multiple lacerations of his face and scalp. If he lives, and right now I don't see how he can live, he will need repeated surgery."

"You've put him to bed?"

Dr. Cornel nodded wearily. "For now, yes. Will you excuse me? I have to talk to the family."

He talked to the family and to the police. A large, grave-

127

faced doctor in crisp, clean whites, he made his evening rounds; he wrote his night orders; he again went into Mc-Clung's room.

The other doctors were catching up on their office appointments and duties.

At a quarter of five it was a group of tired men who gathered in the doctors' room. Cornel decided that he might not get home for some time, if at all that night. But just now he needed to unwind.

Dr. Ruble filled the coffee cups. The men sat with them in their hands, Dewey, head back, in a deep chair, Bob and Garde on one of the couches. Dr. Cornel sat on the corner of the table, his right foot dangling. They talked about the accident and guessed whether a seat belt might have saved the man.

"He wouldn't have been dragged a hundred feet along concrete!"

"But I understand the top of his car was sheered off."

"Knocked back . . ."

Cornel was asked what he would do for McClung, should he live. Alison replied, always pointing out that any plans could be only tentative. He said again that this was the worst impact case he had ever seen, let alone handled. He—

The door to the hall opened, and all the men looked around, expecting to see an orderly with a message. Though even an orderly should have knocked.

So should Libby Gillis.

She seemed completely unaware of this breech—and managed to ignore, too, the fact that she had never used the doctors' room before, if, indeed, she had ever been in it. Now, her dark head high, tilted a little to one side, her white coat crisply unwrinkled, she greeted the men gaily and walked over to the coffee urn.

"I thought I'd better have a little conference about tomorrow's surgical schedule," she said, as she put a drop of cream into the cup. She turned then and looked up at Dewey, who had gotten to his feet and was advancing toward her.

"Hi!" she said, flashing her bright, challenging grin. She was entirely assured and would have walked toward the second couch, with every intent of sitting down, but Dewey moved to intercept her.

"Libby!" he said gruffly. "You shouldn't come in here."

She glanced around at him. "Oh?" she asked lightly. "Why not? It says right on that there door yonder—"

"Libby, I am not joking."

Bob and Garde looked at each other. Alison's hand lifted a little from his knee, as if warning them not to interfere.

"This is the doctors' room," Dewey was agreeing. "And you have your M.D. But you knew when you came here to Bayard that our hospital was not set up to allow you to use this room. The adjoining showers and lockers are not private enough. We—well, we need not discuss the reasons. You should not come in here. You should not *be* in here now. So—scram, will you?" His voice roughened, and his manner was rough.

For a second Libby stood facing him. Then she shrugged. "Well, *excuse* me!" she said. She thrust her coffee cup at Dewey. "You will understand if I don't bother to throw this in your face?"

She turned on her heel and stalked out of the room, her head up, her skirt switching against her handsome knees.

Garde whistled soundlessly. Bob rubbed the back of his neck. Alison's eyebrows climbed his forehead. "Wait till I tell Gene," he murmured.

Dewey set Libby's mug down with a thump that sloshed coffee out on the table and over his hand. He growled and wiped his fingers on his T shirt. "If you have a lick of sense," he told Alison, "you will not mention Libby's name in your home."

Dr. Cornel stared down on the floor. "No?" he asked, his tone only curious.

"No!" said Dewey. "It is bad enough for us to let her

break up our clinic."

"She won't do that," Dr. Cornel said confidently.

Without commenting further, Dewey walked out of the room.

"She could do that," mused Garde, gazing into his coffee cup. "You know?" he said. "I think Windsor was scared."

"He was," said Bob. "I don't think he'd realized how far he has let things go. Someone had to set her straight, and I'm glad Dewey was the one. He'd have resented one of us doing it. And one quarrel a day is enough."

"Oh, what's a quarrel?" asked Alison. "We've always argued."

"Argued, yes. Quarreled, no. Until today."

"You mean at noon? But that wasn't—"

"You and Dewey were not speaking to each other after it."

Dr. Cornel nodded. "I know, but—"

"You think it takes two to make a quarrel. But it doesn't, really. One angry man is enough, and Dewey was angry this noon."

"Yes, I suppose he was."

"We must not quarrel," said Garde firmly.

"No-o," Alison agreed.

"What do you suggest as a means to prevent such quarrels?" Bob asked.

"We didn't used to have such touchiness as Dewey showed this noon."

"And if we'd ask our wives, they would tell us—"

"I think we should not ask our wives anything that would involve a discussion of Libby Gillis," said Bob firmly.

"Who mentioned Libby?" Dr. Cornel demanded.

"It isn't necessary to mention her. Dewey's touchiness—and ours—has developed since her advent in this hospital."

"Maybe you are right," Alison agreed. He sat down in the corner of the couch facing Dr. Shelton and Dr. Ruble.

"That's too bad, too," said Garde, his dark face troubled.

"She is a good doctor, capable in her field, and there should be no personal angle to her service here."

"Maybe there isn't," said Bob thoughtfully.

"You know there is. Dewey acknowledges it by his defensive attitude. He gets mad if we seem to mention the matter, however obliquely, but still he gives us every opportunity to see him with her. He devises means and ways of having her included in our family gatherings. Only last week he had Hazel entertain their bridge group, with Libby invited. Though she has a car of her own, she'll walk to work, then ask to use his car to run an errand, and he lets her. He gives her a lift in that same car—she is seen in his boat. We see them together, others see them—and there is talk. In the town, among our friends, yes, and among ourselves, too. We're talking about it now."

"He must feel guilty . . ."

"Would you say that this has gone far enough that he—"

Dr. Cornel stood up. "Let's stop this!" he said sharply. "Let's stop it and keep it stopped. Or we'll be the ones to break up our clinic!" He walked to the door. "Just *saying* that Windsor is guilty of anything is bad. Talk can—well, let's stop the talk here and now! Shall we?"

Bob shrugged and nodded.

"It's worth trying," Garde agreed.

Chapter 11

THE WHOLE WEEK WAS A DIFFICULT ONE, OF watchful waiting and strain. Alison Cornel stayed long hours with McClung, the man so badly hurt on the highway. He would see him during every hour of the day, go home for dinner, come back in the evening. He would leave home a half hour early in the morning, to check the chart, to study the lab reports, the x-rays, to look up something in a thick book, or sit beside the unconscious man's bed and gaze at him. That the man lived at all—that he survived one day, two, four—was proof of the strength of his heart and his will.

"If he shows the first sign of consciousness," the doctor told the nurse in attendance, "get immediate word to me. And don't leave him alone! Not for a minute!"

"I understand, doctor."

Alison, Gene told the other wives, would have nursed McClung himself. "He is determined to save him. He thinks of nothing else, and the strain on him—on all of us—is terrific."

She wished that McClung might regain consciousness. Then that pressure at least would be lifted. And yet, on the night when the telephone sounded its soft buzz, Gene sat for a second with it in her hand and looked at the sleeping man in the other bed. On his back—completely relaxed—

Should she fib a little? She could say that the doctor was out on another call. The hospital would doubt her word. But she could try saying that and give Alison a few hours' sleep. It was one-thirty—he needed his rest.

But she would not say such a thing! Sacrifice was a part of a doctor's job, no matter how tired he was.

She lifted the telephone again to her lips. "He'll be right over," she told the hospital switchboard.

She set the phone down and snapped on the lamp. Alison roused at once. "Is it . . . ?" he asked his wife.

"Yes. The hospital. McClung is stirring."

In a second Alison was on his feet, into the bathroom, under a cool shower to waken him. He pulled on some clothes, grabbed his bag from the chair, and was out of the room, out of the house—the tires whirred as his car passed the bedroom windows.

Gene sighed. McClung could count on Dr. Cornel. His wife could count on him. She always knew exactly what he would do, how he would respond. And that was a wonderful thing. . . .

She lay back on the pillow and pulled the flower-sprigged quilt up to her chin. She thought about the calm and capable man driving through the dark streets; she thought of the quiet house about her, the table set for breakfast, the bouquet of daisies and little pink roses, the mixer set out ready to make waffles . . .

All in order, safe and to be counted on.

She thought of the girls upstairs in their bedrooms, Susan's untidy, Carol's in order. There were pictures of horses on Susan's walls, pictures of ballet dancers on Carol's— pictures selected when the house was built and furnished. Now, four years later, the girls might select other pictures, though they probably would protest taking these down. They too liked the feeling of continuance, of comforting establishment in their lives. When Gene remembered . . .

She took a deep breath and turned on her side. Alison would not be home very soon. . . .

But the thought of her family and her girlhood remained in Gene's subconsciousness, and on Sunday she spoke again of those things to her friends. That time the men—the husbands—were present.

The four families had all gone to the yacht club for Sunday dinner, a popular thing for members to do. The teenagers sat at their own table, a long and noisy one. The little children sat at another, with special waitresses in charge. The adults thus were free to enjoy their meal, to talk and relax. The view of the river was spread out in panorama before them, the water blue and sparkling in the sun. Speedboats and white-sailed craft, swimmers and a man on skis added to the picture of pleasant leisure.

The eight hospital people sat at their own round table; about them were their friends, ready to exchange a word, to glance their way and smile.

The closeness of the hospital group was recognized and admired. Their friendship was reassuring to the town.

Today the wives had planned this show of concerted strength for the town's sake and their own. They would, they decided on Saturday, go to the club after church, well-dressed and congenial. To be looked at and admired—the young girls in their summery frocks and wide-brimmed straw hats, their little white gloves; Bobby Ruble in his red blazer and white trousers, small Butch Shelton in a replica of the costume.

The men, the doctors, were well-tailored, handsome, and dependable in their summer-weight suits of sharkskin or fine worsted. Their wives—pretty Nan in a red and white printed silk with a small red hat; pretty Ginny in a pale-yellow linen suit and white hat; Hazel handsome in a black and white dress with a snug black jacket, a black veil over her silvered hair; Gene in green, her hat discarded in the car.

The club members and their friends would see them there together, the men talking about McClung, drawing sketches on prescription pads, arguing amiably.

The injured man, they said, should be dead.

But he was not.

"Who performed this miracle?" asked Ginny, in an attempt to draw the whole group together.

"All of us, working together."

"Even *Bob?*" asked Bob's wife.

"He sure was in on it. In fact, he received the case when it first came in."

Ginny smiled softly at Bob, and the others laughed at her expression.

Everyone at the club that day saw the group and recognized the closeness of it.

Libby Gillis had been in the lounge when they came in, and she must have seen all of them; now she was down on the beach, preparing to go water-skiing behind Willard Laurent's boat. She wore a red bathing suit and a white cap.

"Does she belong to any church?" asked a voice within hearing of the doctors' table.

"If so, she never attends."

"Maybe she goes in the winter time."

"I think doctors should go to church. They—"

Dewey Windsor broke a hard roll with a shower of crumbs. Hazel protested mildly. "You don't know your own strength—"

"Why should doctors have to go to church?" he demanded gruffly. "Can't they just be private citizens? And I do mean private. They—" He coughed, his cheeks red, and asked someone to pass him the salad dressing.

Around the table there was a short, and, as it continued, an embarrassing, silence. It was to break in on this that Ginny Ruble blurted her question to Gene. "How," she asked, "did you ever get from your exotic childhood to eating Boone County ham on the veranda of the Bayard Yacht Club?"

Gene looked up, a bit startled at thus having her past brought into focus, there and then. "I wish I'd had more Boone County ham in that childhood," she said grimly.

"You don't have to talk about it if you would rather not," Bob assured her kindly. "Ginny shouldn't be so inquisitive."

"I don't think Ginny is the only inquisitive one in our immediate vicinity," Garde said.

Gene looked around the table at each of the men. Evidently they had been briefed on what she had previously told their wives. Only Alison was unaware of how much she had talked.

"Why have you dug up your—what was your word, Ginny?—your exotic past?" he now asked.

"Childhood, not *past*," Ginny corrected him.

"Is that different?"

"It sounds different. And why shouldn't she tell us about it?"

135

Alison shrugged. "I was only asking why she should."

"I thought—" Gene told him, mumbling a little. "This summer I've had to live it over, and—"

"But need they live it over, too?" her husband asked, his tone mildly reproving.

"Well—no—maybe not," Gene agreed. "But—we share things, and they saw that I was upset . . ." She looked distressed. She wanted Alison to approve of her and whatever she did.

"Of course we share things," Ginny spoke up firmly. "We want to! And now I want Gene to answer my question: How *did* she get here on this porch, one of this not-so-exotic group? In short, how did you *escape?* And what happened to the rest of your family, Gene? There are days—well, I want to know the procedure, for when I may want out."

"Oh, Ginny!" said Hazel mournfully.

Ginny threw her a gamin grin.

"I'll tell you—" Gene began, speaking quickly. Then she stopped, and her face crumpled like a handful of tissue paper. Tears began to run down her cheeks, and everyone exclaimed softly. Nan stood up, but Gene shook her head and dabbed at her eyes with her napkin.

"I'm all right," she told the others. "Go on with your ham. It just suddenly struck me, how normal we are, this bunch. Nothing could be more respectable and—well—so predictable."

"In other words, dull?" drawled Bob.

Gene looked up at the handsome man. His black hair was silver at the temples; his eyes were a deep blue—he was the kindest person on earth. "You are not dull!" she cried tensely. "Our life here is not dull. It *isn't!*"

"All right, Gene," said Alison quietly.

She glanced at him, too. "I'm sorry—"

"You don't have to tell us a thing," Ginny said.

"But I *want* to. It was just—well, the contrast struck me. It will strike you, too, because—you asked what happened to my family. Well . . .

"Pegeen—she was the oldest daughter. Pegeen committed suicide when she was twelve."

"Oh, Gene," murmured Nan.

"She did," said Gene, speaking calmly now. "She walked out into the surf, the way Dr. Boussad had done. Addie—our mother—" Gene glanced across the table at Dewey and Garde. "Our mother had told us the story many, many times and in detail. As if it were a great romance. So Pegeen—

"She left a note saying that she couldn't face being a woman."

"Did you say she was twelve?" asked Bob alertly. Garde was nodding.

"Pressures at that time of a girl's life . . ." said Alison.

"It's a more critical period—" Dewey began.

"Oh, shut up," said Ginny. A woman, passing their table, turned at the tone and looked at her. Ginny smiled brightly and greeted the woman by name.

Then, the outsider safely gone, Ginny looked at Gene again.

"Go on," she urged. "Tell us what *you* did. Your family, we are ready to concede, must have been something to live with."

"It was," said Gene, in a matter-of-fact tone. "It most certainly was. And I did do something about it. Not until I was eighteen, however. But then—then I went to Addie, and I told her that I wanted to study nursing. She—well, at first she laughed at me. Then she patiently explained why I couldn't do such a thing. She had all sorts of reasons, the strongest one being that she was planning my debut for the next winter, and—"

"You?" asked Hazel incredulously.

Everyone laughed; Gene, too. "Me," she agreed.

"But—did you have one?"

"I did," said Gene hardly. "I had a debut—of a sort. It

was at one of those big ball things, with twenty girls all dressed alike. They didn't have me in mind when they selected the gown—I never was the tulle skirt and off-the-shoulder bodice type. Nothing happened, of course, and that same winter I just walked out of the house and got myself a job as a waitress in a big hospital."

"But, Gene—"

"My idea was to pay my way from then on. I didn't know a darn thing that was useful. But I could manage the waitress job, and I planned to save my money, get into a nursing school . . .

"Alison was a med student then, and that next summer he was doing a clinic clerkship. He ate in the dining room where I worked."

"She kept me from starving to death," Alison contributed. "On the money I was getting—a dollar a day, as I recall . . . Sure I fell in love with the girl who brought me three extra pancakes and hid some extra slices of bacon under them."

"How romantic," sighed Dewey.

"It was romantic," Gene assured him earnestly. "Alison was enthusiastic about his work—he'd talk to me. We'd meet when I was through for the day, take a walk, and he'd talk. I'd never met a man, a person, like him. The way he'd study a subject until he knew all about it, the way—"

"All right," Bob broke in. "We get the picture. Romantic Cornel—did he have hair then?"

They all laughed merrily, and even their own children looked their way.

"You should have seen me," said Alison. "And Gene, too. What a scared rabbit she was then."

"Oh, my," groaned Garde.

"It was a wonderful time," Gene insisted. "You birds have no idea. For the first time in my life I could plan on what I would do the next day and do it. I had my own room at the Y. It was tiny, and hot—but no one ever opened that door and came in, except the maid who cleaned. I could leave that room in the morning and come back at night and find it all quiet and safe. Alison—well, he was much as he is now. And you know about *that!*"

"Yes, *ma'am!*" Dewey agreed with her.

"Well, it wasn't bad," Gene assured him. "And it isn't bad now." She smiled at her husband. "He was a big young man, strong, calm—"

She broke off and sat gazing down at the little sailboat tacking off across the river basin. "I never went home again," she said softly.

"That next fall—Alison had told me how to apply and all —that fall I entered the nursing school. At Christmas— my first Christmas on my own—he took me home with him. His family lived in a small town, in a frame house. His mother was—oh, I know many of her sort now. Then, it was the first time I had ever met, or been with, that sort of woman. Gray-haired, a little plump, glad to have her family at home, glad to have her son bring a girl into the crowded little house. She had baked and planned. I slept in Alison's room—he got the couch on a sort of sun porch. We trimmed a Christmas tree. It—well, it was a small home, and orderly. We got up at a fixed time, and meals were served at certain times, and before every meal grace was said. We went to church on Christmas Day. There was a well-used Bible on the living-room table.

"It—it was a new world to me. Breakfast and lunch and dinner—I was allowed to help with the dishes, and they were put into neat cupboards. There were no servants, but there were two aunts, an uncle, and four cousins who came for Christmas dinner. Alison's brother and his sister-in-law—"

"I can just see you," said Ginny.

"They all looked you over . . ."

"They were very kind," Gene said fiercely. "I—they made me feel one of them. It was like—well, like putting on

139

a good warm coat—when you've been shivering in chiffon.

"That week, for the first time in my life—and I am not exaggerating—I could go to bed, sleep deeply, wake in the soft darkness, and feel safe."

For a long minute everyone looked hard at things other than Gene and Alison, who had put his hand on his wife's arm. Down on the pier a girl in a white cap, a man in khaki slacks, knelt on the boards, consulting a spread-out map. A girl in a red jersey and striped capris, armed with a fishing pole and a picnic basket, joined a young man stowing gear into a canvas duffle bag. A cooler, a radio—they were ready for a long afternoon on the river.

When attention again turned her way, Gene was blushing. "When Alison," she began shyly, "when he became an intern, we married."

"Ten dollars a month, and two changes of whites a day laundered for free. My meals," Alison explained. "Oh, we were in great shape!"

"We were!" Gene insisted. "I was working, and I had a wedding. I've always been glad. His mother died the next year. Three months before Carol was born. The war had come, and Alison got a commission—"

"Best residency a man can serve," Alison growled.

"For us, we were rich," Gene admitted. "Even after he went overseas, I could manage on what he allotted me. It was wonderful, though Susan was born while he was away, and strangers—I mean, not family—they were friends, of course!—we wives of the Base Hospital Unit stuck together! One of these girls took care of Carol. It wasn't easy, maybe, but it was wonderful.

"Alison came home safely enough and took a residency. We had quarters right in the hospital. Then we came here. Do you remember that first home we lived in? Ceilings sky-high, the awful bathroom—that tub on feet. I needed a ladder to get into it."

"And the fire department to get you out!" Alison laughed.

140

"Yes, and remember the time the basement flooded? Oh, dear."

"But it was wonderful?" murmured Ginny.

"It was!" Gene insisted. "Then, building our new house ... Can't you, all of you, understand why I have been, why I am, overly conscientious about the home we have, the way my children are raised, and even about my husband? I'm sure Alison thinks I am too tense—I want him to take vacations; I want him to get out in the sun—he tells me to let him alone. But—well, I do nag at him and at the girls—"

"Oh, you don't," Alison assured her.

"You often tell me that I do. Ginny tells me to let Carol alone, and—"

"We are all idiots," declared Ginny.

Gene smiled. "Well," she said uncertainly, "I'll admit that I have been a little over determined to make of my marriage the 'sacred pattern' my father called it."

Everyone stared at her. "Your *father?*" asked Hazel.

"Was he joking?" asked Bob Ruble.

"No," said Gene. "He was being bitter. And maybe even wistful. You know, he was a young man during my childhood. A very young man."

Chapter 12

"WHERE'S DEWEY?" ALISON CORNEL ASKED, COMING into the staff dining room for lunch. He was ten minutes late, and Bob and Garde were finishing their soup.

Bob shrugged. "I saw him about ten."

"I've seen him during the morning, too. Was he called?"

"You could ask the desk," Dr. Shelton suggested.

"Now, if it were you," said Bob, reaching for bread, "I'd say you were looking at McClung. Again."

"I did look at him," Alison agreed. "That's why I'm late. Does Windsor have a critical?"

Garde laughed and glanced at Bob. "There's Mr. Myer," he reminded the Chief of Staff.

"I would not hang around him for very long," Cornel decided. "He's the grouchiest. He sent for me, you know, and protested at Windsor's hospitalizing him. Said he hadn't had a real bad heart attack."

"He hadn't," Garde agreed.

"But Windsor's the doctor. I told him that."

"Make him happy?"

Dr. Cornel laughed. "You know it didn't. In fact, I got a definite impression that his relationship with his doctor left much to be desired."

"To speak mildly," agreed Garde. "Did you hear what happened this morning?"

"To Myer?"

"Well, no. More to Windsor. He told me about it right after it happened, and he looked fairly upset. Shaken would be the word."

"So, tell it," suggested Dr. Cornel.

"I'm going to. You remember that we have a new night supervisor?"

"I keep in touch," drawled the Chief of Staff.

"Good for you! Well, it seems that when Dewey came in this morning and checked the charts, he found written on Myer's, 'Patient not feeling well; complained of some S.O.B.' That shook our Dewey up a bit."

"It should." Alison continued to look interested.

"Dewey hunted up the night Head and asked her—meekly, he claims—"

"Ha!" said Bob.

"I thought it was probably an overstatement." Garde's black eyes twinkled. "Anyway, he asked the Head if he were the S.O.B. referred to. He says she blinked like an owl, then laughed her head off. Finally she explained to him that

142

S.O.B. was her abbreviation for shortness of breath."

Alison chuckled and put a chop on his plate. "Did Dewey have an answer to that?"

"Yes, he suggested that the nurse not put such things in capitals. He said that he didn't like hard jolts first thing in the morning. Who would? Though, you know, patients like Myer . . ."

"Buy our bread and butter," agreed Alison. "Not to mention a few other necessities. Have you heard rumors that the club is going to raise its dues?"

"I'm on the Board," Shelton reminded his friends.

"So you are! Is that true?"

"It's been discussed. Sometimes the revenue drops—you know, not so many parties, fewer people eating at the club, even the concession stand, or bar, if you like. Anyway, their receipts go up and down."

"We must have helped bring them up yesterday," said Bob. "A family like mine runs up the tab. Bobby ate two pieces of pie, I know."

"But then, think—he never gets cherry pie at home."

"His mother asked him if he ever did, and he said, yes, but he was watched too closely at home to have two pieces."

The men laughed and for some minutes ate in silence.

"The things Gene said yesterday," Garde mused aloud, "made both Nan and me take a good look at our home and our family last night."

"Gene—" Alison began.

"She's a fine woman," Bob assured him.

"All our wives are fine women."

"Yes, they are that. With normal faults, of course."

"Would you care to mention some?"

"I might, here in this place and before this company. I don't know that you had better quote me away from this immunity. But I was thinking particularly of the way our girls are ganging up on Libby Gillis."

"Oh, they are not!" cried Garde.

143

"Yes, they are," said Bob seriously. "And they are making entirely too complete a job of it."

"Well, she's ganging up on Windsor, and—"

"One woman cannot *gang!*" Alison protested.

"She can," said Garde, "if she is Libby Gillis."

The surgeon's face was troubled. "She is a fascinating person," he conceded. "But Dewey—you don't mean that that is where he is this noon?"

"I don't know where he is this noon. I said I didn't, and I meant that."

"No reason to get huffy."

Garde leaned forward. "This situation is very hard on Hazel," he said earnestly.

"It's got us all on edge."

"Yes, but—for one thing, she feels the fact that she has no children. She told Nan that it made her older."

"Oh . . ."

"It isn't nonsense if it makes Dewey feel she is older!"

"He doesn't."

"How do you know? A childless marriage—men do stray."

Dr. Cornel snorted. "Then why doesn't she do something to stop him? Why doesn't she make a fight for the man, if she wants him?"

"She wants him all right. But she has a very strong conviction that he has always loved Libby, that he married Hazel only because he was engaged to her and felt obliged to—"

"Maybe he did marry her under such circumstances—I don't agree that he did, but we'll concede that for the sake of this discussion. Maybe, even, he has always loved Libby and thinks he does now that he's with her again—Hazel is still his wife and has things to fight with."

"Maybe you should tell her that."

"I may just do it!"

"Now, wait a minute, Cornel!" Bob spoke up quickly. "Dewey could be really sore if you'd interfere."

Dr. Cornel stood up. "He'd have a right to be sore if I don't," he pointed out. "Now, it's one o'clock, and I'm due at my office."

"Dog days!" panted Gene, trudging up the drive and cutting across to the paved patio where Hazel and Nan sat, watching Ginny Ruble vacuum the swimming pool.

"Did you walk over?"

"No, I did not. Carol dropped me off at the corner. She was going on to pick up Mary at the tennis courts."

Ginny looked across the pool at her visitors. Over her swim suit Gene wore an old terry jacket of Carol's. Nan, in pink gingham, had brought a bulging beach bag and the two children who now were playing in Sarah's sandbox.

"Do you want to swim?" Ginny asked blandly, kicking a snorkel mask out of her way. She wore a white blouse and plaid shorts; her feet were bare.

"Sure we want to swim," Gene told her. "How long . . . ?"

"Bobby should be doing this," Ginny called. "But I told him I would if he'd let Alison look at what I think is a plantar wart on his foot."

"If it is one," Gene predicted dourly, "Alison will do more than look at it."

"I know he will. So—I am vacuuming. I'm almost through. Why don't you go to the beach?"

"The river is full of boats and people," said Nan. "I can't swim there on days when I have to watch the kids."

"And my stomach sticks out," Gene added.

Hazel sat straight up. "What does that have to do with it?" she demanded.

"You wouldn't ask that if *your* stomach stuck out," Gene pointed out.

"I still can't see—"

"Then I'll tell you. Libby Gillis is as apt as not to be down there, and her stomach doesn't!"

Without another word, Hazel lay back in the long chair.

Nan made warning gestures at Gene, and Ginny came

around the rim of the pool to join the group in the chairs beyond the fence. Her face was flushed, and she rubbed the back of her forearm across it.

"Bob's going to cover the pool next winter," she announced, apropos of nothing, but she hoped that the remark might serve to change the subject to safe channels.

"What sort of cover?" asked Nan obligingly.

"The men are discussing it," said Ginny. "They've already had a session with catalogues, and last night a pool salesman was here."

"Bob called Dewey over," said Hazel, her head back, her eyes closed. "Everybody is anxious to close our ranks against Libby and prevent even the mention of her name." Her tone was dry.

"Oh, Hazel!" Ginny protested.

Hazel recrossed her long legs at the ankles. "It's all right," she said. "I appreciate it. Dewey came home last night and talked to me for ten minutes about pool covers. There are various kinds, and they cost various sums, and—Oh, the heck with it!"

Ginny shrugged. "We still mean to cover the pool. Bob thinks it will save work in the spring. You know—leaves and balls and things won't get into the pool. I believe the men favored a custom-made one of plastic mesh that will roll out and over—it could be used even in the summer. It would let rain water through. If you get a solid cover you have to siphon off snow and rain."

"And then there are the new disposable ones," drawled Hazel.

"Yes, there are," Ginny agreed brightly, choosing to ignore her friend's acid tone. "You should have heard that poor salesman!" She giggled. "You would be amazed at all the things we should do that we don't."

Nan came back from settling a small disturbance at the sandbox. "What sorts of things?" she asked, sitting down. "You always drain the pool, and—"

"But we shouldn't drain the pool," Ginny instructed them. "It seems that some water should be left in to prevent cracking."

"But I'd think—"

"So did I. But it seems it is necessary to counterbalance the pressure of the earth against the concrete sides of the pool. Or something."

"How much water should you leave in?" asked Gene. "Not that I care terribly."

"We *should* drain it below the vacuum and inlet fittings, about fifteen inches below the overflow. And we could put a couple of logs in the water."

"For heaven's sake, why?"

"Oh, it's a matter of ice expansion, and the logs would have to be fixed so that they wouldn't bump the pool side."

"My!" said Hazel.

Ginny giggled. "We do drain our pipes and plug the fittings," she announced. "Bob thought the pool man was disappointed to know that we were doing that. Then there was a lot about sand and gravel filters and the care of same."

"Do you even have one?"

"Of course we have a filter, Nan. And we take care of our equipment, too, though not anything like the way this man said we should. Goodness, it would take a storehouse as big as our own house to do all he said. I told Bob I was awfully glad that we had never put in a diving board. Because, sure as anything, we'd have the thing in the living room all winter."

"I think your other idea is better," said Hazel, not opening her eyes.

"What idea was that?" asked Ginny.

"To use the river. *Your* stomach doesn't stick out."

"We have fun in Rubles' pool," Gene defended the project. "It's wonderful for the children. If my family had done things like this—built a pool, you know, and stayed in one place long enough to get some friends like us—"

"Where would you *ever* find friends like us?" Hazel drawled.

"Oh, Hazel, for heaven's sake!"

She sighed and sat up in the chair. "I know. I'm sorry. You're all wonderful. And I am grateful that you want to help me—from what I can only guess. But there are times when I want to crawl into a hole." She lay back again. "Go on, Gene," she urged. "Talk about your family. Then even I will think about something besides . . . Well, anyway, *talk!*"

Gene looked at Ginny and at Nan. Her eyes were troubled.

"Maybe I should never have started talking about them," she said diffidently.

"Of course you should!" cried Ginny. "Bob was saying just last night that it had done you good to talk, that it was much better to bring things out in the open than damming them up in your mind. You were worried this summer—"

"I still am worried," Gene confessed.

"I know it. Look! I'll go in and get some cookies for the kids and something cold for us to drink. Don't say a word until I come back."

Nan followed her, small "Fiddle" showing an inclination to trail her mother. Gene got up and brought the little girl back to the paved terrace. "Mommie will be right back," she comforted the child. "Cookies!"

"Me, too?" called Butch from the sandbox.

"Cookies for everybody!" Gene promised largely. "Sarah, you've torn your pants."

"I know it," said Sarah Ruble unconcernedly. "I'm growing out of everything! Mommie says it's most esspensive."

Gene chuckled, and so did Hazel—unexpectedly.

"I should have about five kids," she explained to Gene. "Then I'd not have so much time to fuss over Dewey."

"He'd be busier, too," Gene agreed. "But imagine you—and him—with five kids! Oh, mercy!"

She diverted Nan and Ginny with this concept while the cookies and lemonade were being distributed. They man-

aged to make Hazel laugh aloud at some of their specu-
lations.

"Go on and talk about *your* family, Gene!" she cried at
last. "I've had all I can take of mine."

"It did you good to talk about your twins!" Ginny assured
her.

"That's what you said about Gene."

"I know I did. So go on, Gene."

Gene nodded and put her glass down on the terrace stones.
"It may help to get things out," she said slowly. "But I had
more peace when I was shutting the other side of my life
away. It was quite enough to live in the present, with Alison
and the girls—and you."

"But it's out now, and if you're still thinking about it, maybe you should tell the rest. If there is any more."

"There is. Some. I don't know how significant any of it
is. Dr. Bailey thought it was important to Shawn's case."

"Your situation is entirely different from his," said Nan
firmly. "I don't think it is at all necessary to seek to tie your
past into *your* present."

Gene smiled wryly. "Maybe not."

"It isn't!"

For a long minute Gene sat silent. A little breeze blew a
yellow-and-blue ball into the clean water of the swimming
pool. Sarah and Fiddle were laughing merrily about something. Butch methodically worked on a sand castle. Down
the hill two squirrels chattered.

"Well," Gene began, "I think I talked about my leaving
home when I was eighteen."

"You did," said Nan approvingly.

"Yes." Gene sighed. "And since then—I've not kept
closely in touch, but I know that things have not bettered
with the family." The muscles about her mouth were tense.
"Because there was—there still is—that age gap between my
mother and my father. When I left home, remember, my
father—Mike—was forty-one, an athlete, handsome,

vigorous, and *young*. He really was. We children always thought of him as more nearly our age than—well, our mother. Addie, for all her efforts, was always old to us. She knew it and hated us for taking such a position. When I left she was fifty-four, dieting rigorously, spending hours on her skin, dyeing her hair—"

"Everybody dyes their hair, Gene."

"They didn't twenty years ago. Not everybody. Of course, for a professional woman, it was accepted. But in the bright sun, which my father loved, Addie's hair—and her skin— showed up unfavorably. She knew that, too. It made a difference between them. She was fighting the old age which lay ahead of her, and she was bitter about what the years could do—what they had already done to her.

"Now—" Gene broke off and sat gazing at the rippling blue waters of the pool. The bobbing bright ball drifted against the far wall. The children in the sandbox were singing a hymn learned in Sunday School, their voices as delicate as gold wire.

"Your mother is still famous," said Ginny softly.

Gene nodded. "Yes," she agreed. "And then—twenty years ago—she certainly was. But still, some of their trouble—hers and Mike's—was due to money.

"Addie's parents had left her some, and she earned the rest. In fact, she earned a great deal of money. With her profession, I mean. She played in concert sometimes as much as nine months of the year, and even after the regular concert season there would be an engagement, or a short tour, in the summer. To Edinburgh, to Tanglewood—or to South America. Her fees were very large.

"My father—Mike—he was not a lazy man, or an indolent one. But I can remember his working only once during the years I knew him. And that time Mother's money had bought him into a business. It had to do with the sale of oil and petroleum products. He had an office—I was taken there once so pictures could be made of his family. There

150

was a big desk and a thick carpet and windows from floor to ceiling, and when I went to them, my toes curled, because the street was so far down below me. Like my sisters, I wore a white sailor dress and a straw hat with a blue ribbon down my back. My hair was long and hung straight.

"Well, anyway, Addie had provided Mike with that office and his business, and she kept reminding him of that. So he gave it up, and they quarreled terribly about it. Of course, they quarreled terribly about all sorts of things. They—"

She broke off, and Nan, a flurry of pink gingham, ran for the sandbox because Jan Ruble had come clattering up the drive on her tall buckskin horse, followed by three of her friends on their horses.

The horses and the eleven-year-olds would be careful not to go out of bounds, but the little folk were not so predictable. Especially Fiddle, who was fascinated by all animals.

It took a good ten minutes for Ginny to welcome the riders, to suggest that they go on through to the pasture, or else, fortified with cookies and lemonade—

"But, Jan, don't track up the kitchen. Mag just scrubbed and waxed it. Of course she will make you lemonade if you go at it right . . ."

This foray successful, the mounted band moved on again, Jan promising to be home by twelve-thirty.

Nan brought Fiddle back to the terrace with her, and the baby leaned sleepily against her mother's arm and shoulder while Nan urged Gene to go on talking. "You were saying that your father and mother quarreled about money. Though even Garde and I do that."

Her friends hooted.

"But we do," Nan insisted. "I'll buy a refrigerator for the Cuban family which the church—"

"A *refrigerator!*" cried the others.

Nan's cheeks were pink. "It was secondhand, and they needed one," she explained. "Of course, it did crimp our budget, and Garde pointed that out. But last winter he

bought an ear-looker-in for his medical bag, and that—"
She joined in the laughter, her expression somewhat
ashamed. "I made too much fuss about that," she admitted.
"But it did make me change my plans for Christmas."

"And you were provoked with Garde about it," said Gene
mildly. "Perhaps I shouldn't even mention to you the sort
of quarrels which took place between Mike and Addie. Over
money, over—well, of course Mike wasn't faithful to Addie.
We called our mother that, you know. I can remember Pegeen, one summer—she was about ten, maybe—and she
made the complaint that other kids she knew had mommies
and daddies. But all she had was Addie and Mike."

"Poor kid," murmured Ginny. Nan kissed the top of Fiddle's curly head.

"Yes!" said Gene. "Even as a very little girl, I knew about
my father's *friends*. In detail. Sometimes I even met them.
They weren't—bad. I mean, they were likable women. I
liked them.

"And Mike—he was a nice guy, you know. In spite of
everything he did and that was done to him. The tragedy
of our home, of all the things I have been telling you, is *his*
tragedy. And has been. I am very sure of that. Nothing that
happened to any of us could equal what went on, and on,
happening to Mike. Not even if Shawn may—prove—to—
be . . . Not even Pegeen's suicide, or even what has happened
to my other sister, Kate. She's been married three times, you
know. And last winter I read in some slick magazine that
Addie Burke's daughter was the gayest woman this side of
Suez. That columnist sure as dickens wasn't writing about *me*.

"But if Addie read that word about Kate, I am certain
she was proud of it." Again Gene stared out across the pool.

"Bob," said Ginny, stirring in her chair, "wants to buy
one of those rattan bath chairs for this patio. You know?
They have sort of hoods? And they are used at European
beaches. He can get one, he says, from Hong Kong for sixty-
five dollars."

"Oh, let him have it," Hazel told her.

"To put here on this terrace?"

"Well, I don't think it should go down on the river beach."

Ginny laughed. "He'll probably get one. Or, maybe, get rattan and expect us to make one. Gene, are you going to swim?"

Gene stirred and looked at Ginny as if surprised to find her there in the chair beside her. "Yes," she said vaguely. "I came over to swim. Is the pool ready?"

Ginny laughed. "It's been ready for the past hour. Wait, I'll change and go in with you."

Chapter 13

A MONTH AGO THE DOCTORS HAD SAID IT COULD NOT happen, but on that warm, breezy August morning the staff of the Bayard Hospital and Dr. Gillis were gathered in the conference room to discuss surgery on Mr. McClung, who had been so badly injured in a highway accident and should by all diagnostic rules be dead.

X-ray plates hung against illuminated panels; there was a blackboard on which Dr. Cornel was sketching the rough-lined skeleton of a man, talking as he worked.

"It is hard to know where to start," he admitted. "But I truly believe our best bet is first to lift and repair the rib cage. We can't do any extensive orthopedic surgery unless the man's respiration is somewhat normal. What about the heart and kidney picture, Windsor?"

Dewey stood up and Dr. Cornel sat down. Dr. Ruble and Dr. Shelton were sharing the conference as the probable second surgeons. Of course the anesthetist would feature largely.

Outside the windows bushes were being tossed about in the

brisk little wind and, blowing, cast their shadows across the parquetry floor, upon the white coats of the people who sat around the table.

Libby Gillis was asked to decide on what her program would be for the first operative session. She answered in a crisp, efficient manner, and the men nodded approvingly. Libby knew her job.

"I'd hope McClung could count on being allowed to go home between surgical sessions," Garde said. "He seems to be hospital-bound right now. Does he know how much surgery he faces?"

"I've talked to him about it," said Dr. Cornel. "And I've explained that we cannot do it all at once. Eventually there must be a bone graft . . ."

"And skin grafts, too, for his face," said Bob.

"Yes. But when this job is over, I do think he might go home briefly, and in a wheel chair, of course, with a nurse. If that would help. After we get to work on his face, he might go home more comfortably and in a more satisfactory manner. The thing is, he has insurance for his hospital stays, and at home there isn't much of anyone to do for him. His wife has taken a job, you know."

"He worries about his parents," said Dewey. "In talking to the man, I've decided that he is an unusual man—son. His parents are not young, of course, and he feels responsible. Not for their care as much as for their peace of mind."

Garde Shelton shook his head. "It is a strange commentary to call a son unusual because he wants his parents to know peace of mind."

"Oh, but—" Libby began.

"I think," Bob said before she could continue, "that most men—and women—are concerned about their parents. Maybe in a tough, defensive manner—the 'I didn't ask to be born' line. But the man who doesn't write to his mother is conscious of guilt feelings, and the son who has not lived up to his father's dreams has the same—or similar—reactions.

Even where our parents are dead we have them on our consciences. If we've failed them, or if they have failed us. If they have succeeded in keeping the relationship good—if we have. McClung is a man able to express his feelings about his parents. Not all of us can do that. Or we don't."

"Except Gene, lately," said Dewey idly. "Of course she seems to have a strong father complex."

Each of the three men turned on him sharply. "Shut up, will you?" rasped Garde Shelton.

"For Pete's sake . . ." growled Bob Ruble.

Dr. Cornel broke the piece of chalk in his hands, looked at it, and threw the pieces, clattering, into the wastebasket. "I concur with Shelton," he said angrily. "This is not the place to discuss staff personalities."

Dewey's face was scarlet, and he slammed his right fist into the palm of his left hand. Libby looked from one man to the other, her eyes widening.

"What goes on?" she asked.

No one answered her. Alison picked up a fresh piece of chalk. Dr. Shelton stacked the x-ray films, and Dr. Ruble took out a handkerchief and blew his nose. Dewey now was holding his head in his hands.

"I'm the world's dumbest cluck," he muttered.

Libby stood up. "I think I could be excused," she said in her clear, bell-like voice. And she walked to the door, through it, into the hall. No one watched her or protested the move.

The door finally closed. Then Dewey said, "I am sorry, fellows. I should not have said what I did."

"No, you should not," Bob told him gruffly. "With an outsider present—"

"I know it," Dewey agreed. "And I am apologizing."

"Make your apology to Cornel," Garde suggested.

Dewey now began to look angry as well as contrite. "I do, if that is what it takes."

Dr. Cornel nodded his head stiffly. "Let's get back to work."

155

"I said—"

"I know what you said, Windsor. But what you said about Gene is not true."

Dewey gaped at him. "If it were true," he cried, "it wouldn't necessarily be bad."

"I consider Gene as well-adjusted as any of the other wives," said Alison, his tone showing affront. "She has her problems, but who doesn't? For instance, Hazel, lately—"

"Suppose we leave Hazel out of it," said Dewey tightly.

"Why in hell should we? If you can diagnose my wife, why can't I state an opinion on yours?"

Dewey sat for a minute looking at the chief surgeon and at his friends. Then his shoulders sagged. "I suppose you could," he said wearily. "I . . . But don't let us quarrel."

"That is strictly up to you," Dr. Cornel told him, turning his back on Dr. Windsor.

Dewey looked at Bob and at Garde. "We shouldn't quarrel," he told them.

"No, we should not," Garde agreed. He spoke calmly.

Dewey got up from his chair; he walked to the window and gazed out of it. He came back. "Look!" he said. "Maybe we should talk about this thing. It could be more important to us, in conference here, than McClung or any patient."

Garde and Bob looked at Alison, who, after a slight pause, turned and came to the chair at the end of the table. "All right, Windsor," he said, his tone still cold, and his face angry. "Talk."

Dewey nodded. He did not sit down but came to stand behind the chair, his hand rubbing across the bent wood of its frame. "I—" he began. "I think the crux of our trouble —the reason we are touchy with each other lately—is the presence of Libby Gillis here in our midst. I will agree that I should not have mentioned Gene's affairs before her. That was a bad slip, and I am shocked that I should have made it." He glanced at Cornel.

"Go on," said Alison, his face relaxing somewhat.

"Well, we have had other run-ins this summer. It has been like a game of touch football around here. And that isn't the way our organization has worked in the past, and it is not the way it should be working now. Heretofore we have been a well-oiled machine, liking each other, doing our work in unison, and considering it to be good work.

"Now if Libby's presence is what is causing the change, I am to blame."

"It takes two," Garde spoke up, "and sometimes four."

"It does, Shelton. But I did bring Libby in here. I thought she was needed here."

"She was needed," said Bob. "She still is needed."

"Not if she—if her being here—will split up our clinic."

"It won't."

Now Dewey sat down in the chair. "It could, Bob," he said, "the way things have been going."

"Yes," Bob agreed quickly. "It could. And it will if you'd forget again and make your comments before the outsider."

"I said I was sorry. I'll try not to let the thing happen again. But I see now that, if Libby stays with us, we are maybe going to have to separate our professional and family interests a little more sharply."

"She should stay," said Alison. "She is a good doctor. She knows her field. And we need her."

"We do need her," said Garde Shelton. "I think all of us should keep that fact firmly in our minds, even when—" He broke off and coughed.

"Even when we hear gossip about her," said Dewey dryly. "And about me."

"You said it. I didn't."

Dewey nodded. "Plenty are saying it," he pointed out. "And there is some basis for the talk."

"What are you saying?" demanded Dr. Cornel, his head snapping up, his jaw jutting.

Dewey put up a conciliatory hand. "Let me say it," he suggested. "The talk says I see too much of Libby, that we are seen together—things like that. And some of that talk is true. And behind that truth is the fact that Libby, from the first, has leaned upon me in this new place as the one familiar to her, the one she knew before coming here, the one she feels she has a claim upon."

"That's her side of it," drawled Bob.

"Yes. Now, as for my side, I have felt responsible for her. I brought her here. I hoped she would like us and want to stay. As you've just said, we needed her. I'd have done the same for a new male doctor."

"But the trouble is, Dewey—"

"I know damn well what the trouble is!" Dewey cried. "I get told it by all my well-meaning friends! Libby is a girl-type doctor, they point out, and I've been too damned kind to her. So, I should, maybe, have slapped her down— in a strange place, an old friend—"

"Now, Windsor," Bob protested, "nobody is saying you should not have been kind to Libby—if that is all there has been to it. Or that you can't continue to be her friend if that is all there will be to it."

Dewey was sitting ramrod straight in the chair, his hands on the table before him. "I mean it to be all," he said quietly. "I mean—it—to—be—all." His face was like marble, carved into lines of grim determination.

Again Bob stacked the x-ray films. "Have you told Hazel?" he asked, almost indifferently.

Garde and Alison leaned forward a little to catch the reply. Dewey rubbed his hand down along his cheek.

"No-o," he said slowly. "I haven't talked—to Hazel."

"I am afraid there has been—and is—a bit of trouble there," said Bob.

Dewey nodded. "I am sure there is."

"Why don't you tell Hazel what you have just told us and go on to straighten the whole thing out with her?"

"That sounds easy, doesn't it?" asked Dewey. "And you can't imagine how often I have told myself that it would be easy. Just go to Hazel—or choose some time when I am with her—and talk about Libby and me—and her. Hazel. But you chaps don't *know!* In the first place I wouldn't know where to start. Hazel and I never mention Libby's name to each other any more."

"You had better mention it now," said Alison firmly.

Dewey nodded, looking down at his hands and the table top. He reached to take a pencil between his fingers. "I need help, Cornel," he said, his tone anguished.

"I am pretty sure," Dr. Cornel said, standing up, and gesturing to Bob and Garde that they would leave, "in fact, I am entirely sure that Hazel will be glad to give you any help you need."

He followed the others out of the room. Dewey sat on at the table, and after a minute or two his head began to nod up and down.

During the afternoon Dr. Windsor kept his usual office hours, and after them he made his rounds of the hospital, going conscientiously from bed to bed, stopping in the hall to speak to the technician with her test tray, conferring with Dr. Gillis across the bed of a young woman patient who was to have her tonsils out the next morning. His white coat was unwrinkled, his manner quite as usual—interested in his patient, asking his questions.

"Did you enjoy your lunch?"

"Is your bed comfortable?"

He was ready to listen to the replies and comment on them, ready to laugh and to make the patient laugh. He admired the flowers beside one bed; he spoke of the bed jacket which adorned the woman who probably had gallstones. He took up her chart and read it. He read the chart of the occupant of the second bed in the room. He told the women, confidentially, that he was going to have to start a class in penmanship in this hospital. "I'll be my own best pupil," he admitted grinning.

He moved down the hall, his heels cracking under his swift progress, and exchanged a quip with the nurse who came toward him. He went into the room of a woman who had an upper respiratory infection but who was reacting unfavorably to the antibiotics. She greeted him with a gasp of relief and extended her arms. "I have smallpox!" she told the doctor.

He took her wrist into his firm, clean fingers and frowned at the half-inch blisters. "I don't think so, Maude," he said consideringly. "It's more apt to be bedbugs."

"Dr. Windsor!" she croaked, horrified.

He laughed. "It's still another reaction," he assured the redheaded woman. "You react to everything, Maude. And I wish you had picked some doctor other than me."

She looked at him uncertainly. "You don't mean that?" she asked.

He smoothed the bedspread. "No, I don't," he reassured her. "Now, will you sit up and let me—"

Her back showed some blisters, too, and as Dewey listened to her lungs, he frowned over the problem which faced him. "I'll want some more sensitivity tests," he said over his shoulder to his accompanying nurse. She nodded and wrote something on the clip board which she carried.

Dewey smiled at Maude and went on to the next room, where he scolded the burly man who had had a mild stroke and who was giving the nurses a lot of trouble. In the last room he sat down beside the old man and talked to him for five minutes about the corn crop.

Finally he could go to the chart desk, flex his shoulders a little, sit down, and reach for the first chart. He read it; he wrote on it; he put it back.

He had ten patients in hospital and two admissions scheduled for the next morning. It took him a half hour to write his orders. When he finished, the supper trays were coming out and the doctors' room was empty. He showered and changed . . .

"Can't take that smallpox home," he told himself under his breath. He dressed and picked up his bag, went out into the hall.

"Doctor . . . ?" said the nurse at the station. She was holding the telephone out to him.

He stifled a sigh and took it, resting his bag on the desk.

"Has he held one of those tablets under his tongue?" he asked into the phone. "All right. I'll stop on my way home."

He smiled at the nurse, picked up his bag, and went on down the hall, through the back door, and over to his car.

"Dr. Windsor looks tired," said the nurses back in the hospital.

"Dr. Windsor feels tired," Dewey would have agreed with them.

He drove out of the parking lot. He crossed town and made his call on the heart patient. His man was all right. But he needed the reassurance and the advice which Dewey gave him, and his wife must be talked to, patted on her plump shoulder . . .

It was already six o'clock when he drove down his home street and could see ahead of him the white house where he lived with Hazel and their dog, Bitsie. The evergreens were dark and lush beside the front steps. Hazel had red geraniums in bloom in pots along the railing. Dewey put his car beside Hazel's and closed the garage door.

Please God, he would not have to go out again that evening. With so much to do, so much to say . . .

Bitsie was clamoring against the fence of their back yard, and Dewey went through the gate to fondle the dog and to look at the gladioli which were blooming magnificently. He straightened a spike. "Where's Momma?" he asked the cocker. Bitsie ran to get her ball and offered it invitingly. Dewey took it and threw it the length of the lawn. He went to the house door and inside. Hazel had the table set in the breezeway, and she called to him from the living room.

"Do you want a drink before you eat?" she asked. Which

meant, "Will you need to make a house call very soon?"

"I want a drink," Dewey agreed. "And if you can hold supper—"

"I can. It's just soup and crab salad."

Dewey put his bag and his straw hat into the hall closet. He went into the bathroom and washed his hands.

"Bitsie's ball gets wetter all the time," he said when he joined Hazel.

She handed him the tall glass and went over to her chair. Music came softly from the hi-fi—somebody on the piano delicately played something by Chopin. Dewey sat down and sighed.

"Tired?"

"Some. Nothing special, except—"

"Ginny and Gene drove to St. Louis today," said Hazel. "They took the girls."

Dewey looked at her. "They did, eh?"

"I expect it will cost a lot to get them ready for school."

"Mhmmn. You know, Hazel, I've been wondering how I got through my days—one patient after the other—when I also had to—"

"I'd think just the usual fall clothes would do it," Hazel went on, speaking rapidly. "But Gene says that the girls won't take care of their sweaters and blouses and things as well as she does, so they'll need more."

"I used to put in a minimum of two hours a day in o.r.," said Dewey.

"If it were my daughter, I'd have trained her to take care of her things!"

Dewey set his glass into the coaster on the table. Yes, Hazel certainly would have trained any daughter she might have had to—

She was evading talk of the hospital, of his work, and, possibly, of Libby Gillis. She had been evading such talk for weeks. But tonight . . .

"See here, Hazel!" Dewey said firmly. "I want to talk to

you about Libby."

Watching his wife closely, he saw her cheeks pale and her eyes widen. Her hand reached up to the throat of her white blouse. "Dewey—" she said, only breathing the word.

"I know, but I feel we have to talk about her, Hazel! So—sit down again, will you? And listen to me."

"I'll let Bitsie in . . ."

"Bitsie is all right. You sit down now." His voice lifted. "And listen to me."

Hazel sat down. She folded her hands in the lap of her plaid skirt; she tucked one foot behind her other ankle. She looked down at her hands, and she was holding her mouth into a straight line.

"Maybe I know what you are going to say." Her voice was thin.

She did not know! How could she know? Dewey felt his face get hot—and red, he supposed. He took a deep breath in an effort to control his voice.

"I thought perhaps," he began, speaking carefully, "that you did not realize how much Dr. Gillis is needed at the hospital." He paused, but Hazel did not speak. "We do need her," Dewey continued. "She is, and can be, an enormous help to us. If we can keep her."

Again he paused and looked expectantly at Hazel. She said nothing.

"Now, maybe you know that," Dewey said desperately. "But what you seem not to know—or seem to forget lately— is that—well—I can recognize the hospital's need for Libby and yet go on as I have always done, loving my wife, enjoying my home and my friends—and I don't want those things changed, Hazel, or spoiled."

Now Hazel moved. She leaned forward, her clasped hands extended. "Do you really mean that, Dewey?" she asked tensely.

"Of course I mean it! How could you even question the matter?"

Hazel sank back into the wing chair. "I—" she began. Then she sniffled a little and shook her head, as if angered by the tears which had come into her eyes. "Libby Gillis," she blurted, "is a very attractive woman!"

Dewey shrugged. "So are you."

Hazel stared at him. "But—" she gasped. "I am not like her!"

"No, you are not. You—"

"She's on your mind. You think about her. You—you are *aware* of her!"

Dewey laughed—or tried to. It was not a very good attempt.

"You do think about her?" Hazel said again.

"Well—yes," he admitted. "But—"

"And she wants you," said Hazel. "All summer she's been trying to get you."

Dewey could think of nothing to say to that charge. Libby, all summer—yes, she wanted him. She—down on the beach, laughing, boldly challenging; at one of the dances, enticing; here in his own home, pretending to look at a portfolio of prints—her tall, slender body, close to him, her hand, her parted lips—the way she would catch her hand through his arm and walk him off somewhere. She did that at the hospital even. And down on the pier. "Dewey!" she would say, "I have to talk to you!" Even now he could hear that throaty voice. Even now, and here, his pulse jumped.

"I'm not such a prize," Dewey said gruffly.

"She's used to thinking *she* is one," said Hazel. "Men have conditioned her to think that."

Yes. Yes.

Dewey looked across at his wife. "Hazel . . . ?" he said pleadingly.

She clasped her hands together, got up, and walked the length of the room; she touched the violet plant which stood on a small stand table before the window; she straightened a magazine and picked up a paperweight, put it down. She turned to face Dewey who was watching her in concern.

"I am trying to understand!" she said tensely. "All summer I have been trying—to understand how a man feels ... You know? Not only about a woman like that—but about other women. His wife, for one. And it isn't easy to try to think and to feel as a man would do."

"As I would do, you mean," said Dewey gravely.

For a second her blue eyes lifted to his face. She had turned about and stood silhouetted against the window and the greater brightness from out of doors. The room had become shadowy.

"Not only you," she said, her tone that of dispassioned argument. "Because I also have to decide how other men—how most men—feel about women. Their response to them. How deep that response can be, how shallow. Also I have to know in just what way a man feels about his—his other—his former—well, relationships. How important is one set against another. I have to decide if a man just feels, without thinking about—other things."

"A woman would? Think about obligations—and other things, I mean."

"I would," said Hazel. "Yes."

Dewey reached for his glass and drank from it. Perhaps Hazel would think so deeply about those things that temptation would never come her way. In that case it could not be easy for her to understand the emotions which had, this past summer, buffeted the Windsors. Husband. And wife.

Dewey took a deep breath. "The hospital, as I say, needs Gillis. But I—the other men—do have a conscience about obligations and things of that nature, and they would agree to send her away—if—"

"But," Hazel said quickly, *"that* wouldn't be right. Nor fair!"

Dewey took a step toward his wife. "You are a remarkable woman," he said warmly.

Hazel backed away from him. "I am not!" she cried. "I

have been—I am—terribly jealous! And it *is* terrible, Dewey. You cannot imagine! I couldn't sleep. I plan things I would do—that I might do. To her—and even to you. I have been—I am—frightened about myself."

"Hazel—"

"Don't touch me! Not now. I want to be able to think and talk reasonably. I've known that—sometime—you and I would have to talk about this—and about her. I have dreaded it. I have protested against it—to myself, of course. I wish we could have gone on as we were, comfortably accustomed to each other, and satisfied. At least, I was satisfied."

"But I was, too, Hazel. Content. You have to believe that."

"If you say so. But that is why it is hard for me to realize that you could—"

"I've done nothing!"

She looked at him wide-eyed now, and he colored. "I meant—"

"I know what you mean. And the difference is not too important, is it?"

"Yes," said Dewey, "I think it is. Because if you—look! Can't you imagine yourself being attracted by some other man, excited—perhaps not entirely happy about it, but—"

Hazel shook her head. "I can't imagine such a thing, Dewey."

"It could happen, just the same."

"I hope not."

Dewey turned and walked the length of the room; he turned on a small lamp that stood upon the old walnut chest. He and Hazel had restored that chest, working long hours on the project, scraping, oiling, sanding, waxing. Now it was a beautiful piece of furniture. Dewey rubbed his palm across the top it.

"You speak as if—" he began. Then he stopped and tried to say it a different way. "I am not the only man who has been—who is—well, interested—in Libby. And I can truly say to you that I have hoped that she and some other man—"

Hazel nodded. "That could happen," she agreed, "if she knew she couldn't possibly have you."

Dewey showed his surprise. "But she should know—"

"That you are married? That you have a wife and a fat cocker spaniel?"

"Hazel! Don't—don't hurt yourself this way!"

She lifted her hand as if to dismiss any consideration of her hurt. "You are plain stupid, Dewey," she said, "if you think that—that woman—will recognize my rights in this."

"You don't know her. You haven't—"

"I have given myself, and her, every chance for us to know each other. And I do know her, enough. She is interested in you. She is not interested in me. So— my being your wife is not important to her."

"You mean, I should tell her that I couldn't—that I wouldn't—"

"Telling her might not be enough, Dewey. But I think that if you would *show* her how you feel—about meaning to keep your home, you know—the things you said you wanted to keep. But you would have to show her, Dewey. *Prove* it to her."

Dewey considered this. "I'd have to do that, eh?"

"I am sure you would have to."

He sighed. "I am a weak man, Hazel," he said, almost in his usual comically deprecating manner.

But Hazel did not smile. "There is at least one way of making yourself strong," she said, "even where—where Libby Gillis is concerned."

He looked up, alertly interested. "What way is that?" he asked.

"Well, I heard this a little while ago. Some psychologist, or something, advised it. He said, if a person really wanted to cure himself of somebody—infatuation, or even interest, was meant. Perhaps even love. But, anyway, if that person wanted to stop being interested in someone that was not worthy of his attention, or if the interest was not a desirable development—there were two things to do. Things you might do. First, you should compare the unwanted person with—in your case—with every other woman who is admirable and attractive . . .

"I don't know if that approach would work with—on—Dr. Gillis or not," she interpolated, in her blunt, honest fashion. "Because she'd probably show up more attractive than anyone you could possibly think of. But maybe the second rule would apply. And that is this, Dewey:

"Every time you look at her, or think of her, you should also think about something unpleasant connected with her. Pretty soon it will become painful to think about her at all." She glanced hopefully at Dewey who stood, thoughtful.

"Something unpleasant, eh?" he mused.

"Yes. Some mannerism—or maybe some physical thing that faintly annoys you. If you kept noticing *that,* and thinking about it—"

"I see. Hmmmmn." Dewey walked about the room, frowning, muttering to himself. "She's a handsome woman," he said thoughtfully. "But, of course—well—there's a little mole on her left shoulder. That wouldn't be enough—I don't see it all the time, anyway. Hmmmn."

Hazel watched him, apprehension building in her eyes. She should have stuck to her determination not to talk about Gillis! She—

"She does have one habit that is irritating as all get out," Dewey was saying. "You know? The way she rubs her nose when she talks! It isn't too bad a habit, but sometimes it makes her voice twang, and anyway, rubbing her *nose*—"

Hazel nodded. "You can watch for that instead of noticing other things—yes, that little trick might do it."

"Well, I'll give it a try. But in case it doesn't work very well —for me, you know, I'd not be a very good subject for any psychologist!—don't you think we might try some other things? For instance, why couldn't we try to help Willard's cause along? He seems to have fallen for Libby, and he'd be ideal for her. His age is right, and there's all that money." His tone lifted hopefully.

Hazel laughed. "We can help that along," she agreed. "Though honestly, I don't think Willard has a chance with her until she is persuaded that she can't, and won't, have you."

"I tell you I'm no prize!"

"And I tell you . . . Besides, she thinks she can have any man she wants. It's you men who have given her that idea, too."

"Well," said Dewey stoutly, "she won't get me!"

Twenty years ago she had not "got" Dewey Windsor, and he had always, though vaguely, regretted it. Now she might not "get" him—Dewey's promise was worth a great deal. But still, he might—

Suddenly, without warning, Hazel sobbed, and tears poured down her cheeks. She fumbled for a handkerchief; the blouse she wore had no pocket. Dewey brought his to her, mopping her cheeks, pressing her head against his shoulder. Hazel sobbed and sniffled a little . . .

"I know I don't—cry—prettily," she told him, comforted by his warmth and his strength.

"I like the way you cry!" he assured her. "I like almost anything you do, Hazel. And I mean that."

"Well . . ." She half laughed, half sobbed. "You don't have to hunt around for things about me—to dislike."

"I won't," he assured her. Then he looked out across the room, over and beyond Hazel's head. "Will it be all right," he asked diffidently, "if I try to stay away from Libby now? I can, you know."

Hazel straightened. "Yes," she said, "it will certainly be all right. That's mainly what has been worrying me, Dewey. I knew you could stay away from her. You just didn't."

Dewey stared at his wife. And slowly, painfully, a tide of deep crimson swept across his face.

169

Hazel put the palms of her hands against his cheeks, and she kissed his lips. "I *am* trying to understand, dear!" she assured him.

Chapter 14

"THE NEXT BABY THEY BAPTIZE IN OUR CHURCH," said Dr. Cornel, "I hope they don't do it in champagne!"

"Hang-over, Doctor?" asked the o.r. Head.

"Of all sorts. My feet ache, because there is some rule that no man can ever sit down at a cocktail party. I don't like champagne, but Rickham kept filling my glass, so I drank too much before I got smart enough to set the thing down and walk away from it. And food!" Dr. Cornel whirled to face the tall nurse. "If you put out nine or ten platters of goodies—little cheese biscuits, and other biscuits with a wedge of country ham, shrimp on toothpicks, and little shiny sausages, meat balls and chunks of pumpernickel—what do I do? I go the rounds, and if not stopped, I keep going around!"

The nurse laughed and added another green packet to the ones already on her tray. "Nobody stopped you, I take it."

"They did not. And today I am paying for it."

"You must really celebrate a baptism in your church."

"Well, as a matter of fact, we don't. Oh, sometimes the family invites people in for a glass of wine. There will be salted nuts and maybe fruitcake. But these people! *Wheee!* Of course my wife couldn't lecture me or point any morals because she was the one who said I must attend the thing."

"Did she go?"

"Oh, yes. But she has a stronger character than I have."

"Doctor . . ."

"Well, she didn't eat and drink as much. The thing is, I don't like champagne! But, then—" He stood looking at an overlapping series of crudely lettered cards hung above the autoclave. "I don't like the people who gave yesterday's party, either."

"Then why did you go?"

"I find that a man can be rude to his friends, but it is almost never wise to snub the people he doesn't like. For instance, the guy who gave the party is on the staff of our competitive hospital."

"Oh!" said the nurse, as if enlightened about all sorts of things.

"That's it. I don't like those doctors. I don't like the work they do. I don't endorse their reasons for being the sort of doctors they are, but they do belong to our church—this particular man does—and I went to his damn party! Excuse me. Now! Who puts all these little order-signs up in this service room, Mrs. Newton?"

"Well, you put up the one about gloves not being sterilized in the autoclave."

Dr. Cornel chuckled. "I guess I did at that. But couldn't we have these notices and requests made a little more tidily? Maybe one largely lettered bulletin board? These snips and snaps of paper hanging around the room . . . Will you speak to the administrator?"

"Yes, Doctor."

"Good! I'll take that tray with me."

"But, Doctor . . ."

"I still can keep my dignity and carry a tray of surgical packs," Dr. Cornel assured her. "I hope."

He backed out of the room, tray in hand. He walked along the hall, his face thoughtful. He had that cervical injury to see—and that hand—

Unexpectedly Dr. Ruble popped out of the Suspect Room and almost knocked the tray out of Dr. Cornel's hands.

"*Whooops!*" he cried. "I'm sorry, Doctor. What's all that? Your lunch?"

Dr. Cornel grunted. "What have you got in your little

cubby, Bob?"

"Me? Oh, an intussusception. Maybe."

"You think up the nicest things!" said the surgeon.

"Mhmmmmnnn. I wanted to keep the baby on here. The parents took him home for two weeks. Now he's back, skinny as a grasshopper. I'll be in touch with you. Did you get your long distance call?"

"What long distance call?"

"I don't know what call. Just that the switchboard had one for you—person to person."

"And naturally I would be the last to know," growled Dr. Cornel, going down the hall, now walking fast. He'd go over to his office, ask for the call, and attend to it before he saw his first patient. If Bob did have an intussusception, they might do it on an emergency basis later that afternoon. Those things didn't usually wait around . . .

Though maybe Shelton would do a better job. He was exceedingly skilled with infant surgical problems. . . .

Dr. Cornel spoke to the receptionist, smiled at the people in the waiting room, and went swiftly into his own consultation rooms. The receptionist, and now the nurse, told him that there was a call.

"I'll take it at my desk," he said, giving his tray to the nurse. "Get the first patient in and ready, please, Mrs. Keith —and maybe the second one on deck. Dr. Ruble may have some surgery for us later this afternoon."

"The Rosen baby?" asked Mrs. Keith alertly.

"Try and keep a secret around this joint!" growled Dr. Cornel. Mrs. Keith left the room, smiling. Dr. Cornel's bark definitely was stronger than any bite of his.

Dr. Cornel sat down behind his big desk. With one hand he pulled the phone closer; the other fingered the mail on his blotter. Mrs. Keith would have sorted out and put elsewhere all medical journals, ads. . . .

"Do you have a long distance call for me?" he asked the switchboard girl. What was her name? Millie something.

"All right, then," he said. "Put it through!"

He tucked the phone into the hollow of his shoulder and opened one of the letters. A meeting of the surgeons of his wartime hospital team. He would try to attend.

"Are you ready, Doctor?" asked Millie in his left ear.

"Right here."

"All rightie!" said Millie to the distant operator. Cornel must get on her about that! "Dr. Cornel is ready. Here you are, Doctor."

The big man in white laid down the letter and reached for a cigarette. But at the first words into his ear, he dropped the thing, took the phone into his hand, and reached out for his memo pad and a pen.

All summer long they had been waiting for this call from Dr. Bailey.

He listened; he wrote on the pad; he asked a question, and another.

He thanked the psychiatrist. Yes, he would talk to his wife. They would be in touch. Yes, the arrangements should be satisfactory. He felt sure that Shawn's parents—they would *have* to agree! "Thank you, Doctor," he said quietly. "Thank you very much!"

He put the phone down, picked up the cigarette, and leaned back in his chair. All at once he was very tired.

Mrs. Keith's head came around the door. "Sir?" she asked.

"Give me a minute," said the doctor. He would not telephone to Gene. He would get through the afternoon's dressings and examinations as quickly as possible. Shelton definitely could handle that surgery. Alison meant to go home to Gene, and as quickly as possible, to talk to her in person.

The news from Topeka was good. Shawn was responding to drugs. There would need to be six months of hospitalization. Perhaps a year. Still, Gene would worry about whether the doctors were right that Shawn's case was reversible. She would worry about herself and the girls. Her husband, a doctor, must do all he could to reassure her. So . . .

He tipped his chair forward and got to his feet. He'd get the jobs here taken care of as quickly as possible.

It was early for Alison to be coming home, and though she had heard his car come into the garage, Gene still looked up at him in surprise when he came around the porch door.

"Is anything wrong?" she asked.

Alison smiled upon her benevolently. "Is that any way to greet your lord and master?" he asked, coming in.

He nodded at Nan and Ginny, who were sitting on the glider. Ginny in blue, Nan in a red skirt and white blouse, they looked fresh and crisp. Gene wore old denim pedal pushers and a striped shirt with the tail out.

Alison shook his head at her offer of a root beer. "I still have a champagne hang-over," he confessed.

"Is that why you came home early? I mean, are you sick?"

"I'm not sick. I came home when I was finished for the day. And I just don't have any yearnings for root beer."

"We were talking about that party," Ginny told him. "We decided that the Bayard Hospital staff effort was a bit more than was necessary."

Alison sat down on the chaise and put his feet up; he leaned back and sighed luxuriously. "I should do this more often," he said. "Go on, girls. I like to listen to gossip. Excuse me if I don't contribute."

"Don't pay any attention to him," Gene told the other two women. "He has as scooped an ear as anybody."

Alison closed his eyes.

"The Rickhams have a lovely home," said Nan, a bit uncertain about talking freely before one of the men.

"He makes good money," Alison contributed.

"I understand they have a full-time gardener," said Gene. "Their place shows it, too. The grounds are beautiful."

"Do they keep Libby Gillis on that green cot beside their pool full-time?" her husband asked, not opening his eyes. "They should—she made a beautiful picture. What was that Mother Hubbard she was wearing? Silk?"

The women laughed. "The Mother Hubbard, dear Alison," said Gene, "was a shift. And it definitely was silk. The yellow was exactly right for that couch, too. The cushion is foam rubber, you know."

"What cushion?" asked Alison.

"On the 'cot,' as you call it. It has a long cushion of luscious green foam rubber."

"Did Gillis lie there all evening? She looked like a Lorelei or something."

"She did, and she knew it. No, she didn't stay there, because she had that row with Dewey, and—"

Alison opened one eye. "What row?" he asked, his voice deep.

Ginny bounced a little on the glider. "Do you mean to tell us that you men didn't talk about it today?"

Dr. Cornel closed his eyes again. "Monday is a busy day at our hospital," he said pompously.

"For that," said Gene, "we shouldn't tell you about the row."

Alison said nothing, knowing that the women were watching him. But . . . He began to frown. "Did they really have a row?" he asked. "Dewey and—at *Rickhams'*?"

"They did," said Ginny. "Not a big free-for-all, of course. But I heard it, and I suppose everyone out on the terrace did."

"With all that going on," mourned Alison, "I had to stay inside."

"Near the table with the food," Gene agreed. "He didn't sleep last night," she confided to her friends. "After all that bacon rind and cheese delights."

Alison was still frowning. "What did they row about?" he asked. If things had got to the point . . .

"Well," said Ginny, "Dr. Gillis was lying on your cot— and you must have been outside long enough to see her. While she was still there, Dewey brought his champagne glass outside. And when he saw her—as who wouldn't? On

175

her a Mother Hubbard looks very, very good!"

"Tell your story, Ginny," Alison begged. "That telephone could ring, and the next time I see him, I've got to know whether to slap Windsor on the back or jump down his throat."

"I'll tell you if you'll shut up."

"She has rehearsed this story," Nan informed Alison. "I've already heard her tell it twice."

Now both of Alison's eyes were open.

"I told it to Nan as we were driving over," said Ginny hastily. "And to Gene before you came. I know enough not to talk about us to outsiders, Alison. If I didn't, Bob would teach me."

"I hope. So, now tell *me* your story."

Ginny nodded and smoothed a blue-checked ruffle on her skirt.

"Well, it seems that Dr. Gillis—Libby—had taken Dewey's boat out yesterday morning."

"Again?" asked Alison sharply.

"Yes, again. While he was at church. He seems to have told her not to—"

"How could she . . . ?"

"Get the keys? She just asked the pier attendant. And—you know her as well as we do—the pier attendant gave them to her. Dewey was hot about that, too. He really told her off about it, and when she tried to explain—"

"You said 'cajole' before," said Nan.

Ginny flushed prettily. "I know I did. And she did, too. Cajole, I mean. She sat up; she looked earnestly at Dewey and talked, and he—he told her, for heaven's sake, to stop rubbing her nose! She does that, you know." Ginny demonstrated the little mannerism.

"But la Gillis—"

"Don't call her that!" said Alison.

"I'm sorry. *Doctor* Gillis just got a bit more gay and said she thought that 'what was thine was mine.' She said that to

Dewey, you know."

"I understand. Go on."

"Well, he got very red—it even showed through his white hair on his head—and he shouted at her that it was not! Then he quieted down a little and told her that she had absolutely no claim on him or on anything of his. He went on to point out to her that there were some things a man wanted absolutely for his own. His razor, his boat—and his home. With no poaching allowed."

Alison sat up on the chaise. "He said all *that?*"

"He certainly did."

"Well, hurrah for Dewey!"

"Yes, I thought so, too."

"What did Libby . . . ?"

"Oh, she didn't like it. You could tell. But she just laughed a little and shrugged her shoulder. She got up off the 'cot,' looked around at the audience, smiled at Willard Laurent. She put her hand through his arm—he was *delighted!*—and they walked across the terrace to the house. Libby had on pale-green slippers without any backs, and her bare heels went up and down on the high green heel, and Dewey asked me if I didn't think she had mighty big feet."

Dr. Cornel grunted. "Well, he should know about such things . . ."

"Oh, Hazel does!" Ginny giggled, and the others joined in, laughing merrily.

"I should think," Gene mused, "that after his saying all that to her, Gillis wouldn't have much of anything more to do with Dewey, ever."

"You mean you wouldn't," said Ginny.

Gene shrugged. "I'm hardly comparable. In fact, I'm not able to figure out a woman like that to any great extent at all. People like her—the men do, certainly. And if it weren't for Dewey and Hazel, I suspect we would like her, too. But still, she has a rush—a push—a—well, it's almost ruthless-ness—"

177

"I think she has helped us," said Nan unexpectedly.

The others looked at her, Gene and Ginny in protest.

"A fine kind of help she's been!" cried Gene. "All summer she's had Dewey acting like a lovesick kid!"

"And Hazel ready to do almost anything!" Ginny agreed. "And Bob's been worried for fear she would do dreadful things to the clinic. He said you were quarrelsome, Alison—"

"We were. We have been. Because if one word was ever said against Gillis, Dewey would jump down our throats. Yes, she's put things into an uproar a time or two."

"But that's what I mean," said Nan, sweetly firm. "I think an uproar can be good sometimes. I think maybe your clinic —and Dewey and Hazel, too—even the rest of us—can be better for a shaking up. Hazel and Dewey had got used to one another and took each other for granted. Maybe the rest of us had forgotten what it takes to be friends."

Gene stole a glance at her husband and found him looking at her.

"I hope you're right," said Ginny thoughtfully. "That things may be better—"

"I believe she is right," said Alison firmly. He looked at his watch. If Bob meant to have that surgery this afternoon . . .

Ginny and Nan caught the gesture and glanced at one another. "I have to be getting home," said Nan. "Are you ready, Ginny?"

"No, but I'll go with you rather than walk."

It took them another five minutes actually to depart, and then Gene came back to her husband, whom she had been watching during the past half hour.

"Is something wrong?" she asked him.

Alison smiled at her. "Come and sit down," he invited.

"Is there?" She perched on the front edge of the glider cushion.

"Yes," he said slowly. "Well, no—maybe."

"Alison!"

He laughed a little. "It's nothing except that the report from Bailey came in today. At noon. I came home as soon as I could to tell you."

Gene pushed her hair away from her face. "Was it bad?"

"No," he said deliberately. "In fact, it was good. It said that while your brother is definitely schizophrenic . . ."

Gene lifted her hand to her mouth.

Alison continued equably ". . . . his hospital stay is foreseen to be no more than a year. Possibly less. That, as against the dozen years which is average."

"I see." Gene stood up. "I should change my clothes," she said vaguely. "I look terrible."

Alison went over to her and put his arm around her shoulder. "You are not to let this thing disturb you, Gene!" he said firmly.

She shook her head. Her face was troubled but not frightened. "I am not going to let it disturb me," she assured her husband. "This summer I've gone over the whole thing—talked about it, you know. And I am pretty sure I got out in time."

She walked away from Alison and straightened the magazines on a rattan table. "I sometimes act goofy," she mused. "But it's a normal sort of goofiness. You know?" She peered around at the man in his clean suntans. "Women are always a little silly. Even Nan is at times. Ginny goes into terrific spins, and Hazel can get so moody it's awful. But no one thinks *they* are crazy!

"As for the girls—Alison, really, our daughters are so normal it is disgusting. All summer I've been watching them—as against the other girls they know—and they are definitely normal. Take this afternoon. Susan is over at Rubles' catching butterflies in their meadow—"

"Fritillaries," murmured Alison. "For her next year's science project. She's collecting fritillaries."

Gene waved a hand, dismissing his fine distinctions. "Well, whatever—and Carol," she continued her analysis. "She went off with a clothespin on her nose."

"A *clothespin!* You call that normal? Why in Tom Thunder . . . ?"

"She's training her nose. Cornelia told her yesterday that it inclined to the left—or maybe the right. Anyway, she's going to make it grow straight by the end of September. She asked me if I thought you'd operate, and I told her if she mentioned it you would hit the ceiling."

"Consider it hit," said her husband, nodding.

That evening Alison asked Gene if she wanted to drive to the hospital with him, wait while he made rounds—"I have to write my night orders"—and then go on to Rubles' for an hour.

Yes, she would like to do that. She was grateful for Alison's close attention to her that afternoon and for his provision for the evening hours.

"Let the girls clear away the dishes while you go change," said her husband.

Gene looked down at the denim pedal pushers she still was wearing and at the old shirt. "I'm sorry," she said contritely. "I should think more about the way I look. I meant to change."

"Go do it now," said Alison gruffly.

"The trouble with Mom," Carol told her father, as she stacked dishes on a tray, "she never wants to throw away anything old. Even my old clothes, and Susan's—she hangs on to them and wears them."

"What do you suppose we can do about that?"

"Keep nagging at her," said Susan cheerfully. "That's the way she does with me."

"Her nagging only shows how much she loves you."

"Well, wouldn't we be loving her, too?"

Alison laughed and went to see how Gene was getting along.

Around five that afternoon Bob Ruble and Garde Shelton had operated on the baby with the digestive difficulties. So that evening Dr. Cornel and the obstetrician had things to talk about. Ginny and Gene sat on the couch and sorted odds and ends of yarn, sometimes speaking quietly to each other, sometimes listening to what the men were saying. The evening had turned a little cool, and the two dogs—a sheep dog and a dachshund—were sleeping on the hearth rug.

"They hope we'll take the hint and light the fire." Ginny laughed.

From the far reaches of the third floor came the sound of Bobby's trumpet. The two little girls were getting ready for bed, with much scampering about and laughter. "They should make it by nine o'clock," said Ginny.

Mary had a date.

"What are you going to do with all this wool?" Gene asked Ginny, winding some pale-blue yarn around a piece of cardboard.

"I'm going to take up crewel work this winter, and I mean to make my own designs."

"Oh, Ginny!"

"It's beautiful. They frame pieces, you know—use it for footstools, handbags, and all sorts of things. I saw a woman giving lessons the last time we were in the city."

". . . convince the mother that the child can get well. . ." Bob's voice came out clearly. "If a man could just shake some of his patients—"

"Or give them a sound slap," Alison agreed. "It would solve a lot of our problems."

"You never wanted me to spank the girls," Gene told him.

"But you did anyway."

"That's what makes them so well-adjusted now," she said pertly. Then her face paled, and she dropped the blue yarn and its reel into her lap. "I'm going to have to go to New York," she told Ginny.

"Oh? When? Why?" Ginny was instantly excited.

"Gene?" Alison asked anxiously.

"Yes," she nodded. "I decided that while I was getting

dinner. You see . . ." She looked across at Bob, then at Ginny. "We had word from the psychiatrist today—about my brother. He needs treatment for a year. Then he can return home. I want to go to New York and tell my parents. Tell Addie—" Her fingers fumbled for the yarn.

"I don't think it will be necessary," Alison began, still anxious.

Gene looked up at him. "I have to go, Alison!" she said firmly. "There are things to be done. Things I must do. With this second chance."

"You mean . . . ?" Ginny looked appealingly at Bob. "If you have any thought of punishing them, Gene . . ." she cried. "You don't need to feel that way! You should not!"

Gene shook her head and steadily wound the blue wool, pausing to untangle a snarl, then going on, her right hand rhythmically circling her left. "I'm not being vindictive," she said quietly. "But this—this problem to be faced—will panic Addie. She will take it personally, you know. She would have felt the same way if one of us had been born crippled. Like that mother Bob's been talking about. I've seen such women, in the hospital when I was nursing. If their baby was born with a clubfoot or something, they were ashamed. Well, Addie will feel that way about Shawn. So I have to go and tell her what she must do. What she can do. She's too old to face failure—a thing she would consider failure—and handle it. I'll go."

"When?" asked her husband, his voice stern.

"Next week, if I can get things organized. If not, the week after."

Alison shook his head. "That can't be arranged," he said flatly.

"Why not?"

"Because Shelton leaves for Atlantic City on Monday, and he and I never go away at the same time. It leaves the hospital without a surgeon. Bob thinks he can't do anything except Caesareans and hysterectomies."

"I can do 'em. I can't diagnose 'em," said Bob cheerfully.

"I can go alone," Gene pointed out.

"Oh, no, you mustn't," Ginny protested. "Look, I can go with you. I could get away for a few days, and——"

Distractedly Gene looked at her husband for help.

"It is very kind of you, Ginny," Alison said warmly. "But I expect Gene will want you to keep an eye on Susan while she's gone. Then there are the Shelton children."

"Is Nan going with Garde?"

"You know she is," said Gene. "She was talking about it this afternoon. She said she was nervous about leaving the children for two weeks, and we told her we would help Rosebud if necessary. But now—that's another reason you couldn't go with me, Ginny. Hazel is certainly no one to leave our kids with."

Ginny giggled. "Be fun to find out what she would do."

"Fun, maybe," Gene agreed grimly. "But think what it would do to Hazel. No, you have to stay here and help her."

"But——"

"Carol can go with Gene," said Alison calmly. "If she must go."

"Carol!" Gene dropped her reel of yarn. Ginny looked across at Alison, her blue eyes round. Bob leaned forward a little and took the pipe from his mouth.

"*Carol!* To suggest that she would be a help to Gene at such a time of stress . . ."

"Of course Carol," said Alison, still calmly. "She's old enough to go away to college next month. She's almost as old as you were, Gene, when we married. She's a poised young woman, and she'll be both a comfort and a help to you."

Gene continued to stare at him. Ginny touched her arm. "He's right, you know, Gene," she said softly.

Chapter 15

"WE LEFT THE HOUSE IN AN AWFUL MESS," SAID Carol when she and her mother were at last seated on the plane for New York.

"It was that or miss this boat," said Gene. "I hope Father's pills work."

"You're not to think of being airsick!" Carol spoke firmly. "Dad said they would work, and they will."

Gene pushed her hat from her head and settled down into the seat. "You'll get all mussed," Carol warned her.

"Then Father shouldn't have given me pills that would make me sleepy. Besides, this dress is supposed to be wrinkle-proof."

"Wrinkle-resistant. You're challenging it."

Gene looked at her daughter in some surprise. She had, for so long, thought that Carol was emotional, unstable, dependent.

"What's wrong?" asked that daughter.

"Nothing. I'm just realizing that you are growing up."

"At nineteen? I'd hope so. Now, tell me what we are going to do in New York? How long will we stay? I don't want to go up on the Empire State Building, but I do want to see the big ships . . ."

"Do you know where we are going?" Carol asked, as the taxi pulled up at the curb before a row of tall, narrow houses.

"Of course I know," said Gene. She paid the driver and smiled at him. "I used to live here—we owned this house when I was a child." She started up the steps. "It won't be the same, of course. Addie used to do it over every year, or almost." She touched the doorbell. "Shawn told me that she had made it into two apartments. Otherwise I'd just walk in."

Gene jiggled from one foot to the other, and she gasped sharply when one of the wide front doors was opened by a maid in trim black and white. Carol looked anxiously at her mother.

Both she and Gene spoke at once, Carol giving way with a murmured apology.

"Yes," said Gene. "I would like to see Madame Burke. You may say—"

"Madame Burke has already left for the dinner," said the maid, beginning to close the door.

"The dinner?" asked Gene, stepping up to the threshold.

"Yes, ma'am. The dinner in honor of her retirement."

"Oh, is that tonight?" For a swift second Gene was back on the front stoop of home, with a thrush singing, and sunlight—cobwebs on the grass . . . She shivered a little. "Well, is my—is Mr. Burke in?"

"Ma'am, I don't think . . ."

"If you tell him that his daughter Eugenia is calling, I think he will see me."

Carol watched her mother, fascinated. No one ever dared call Gene that. And on top of the "Madame Burke"! Wait till Carol told Susan! And Mary! And—

The maid had been holding the door against further intrusion, but now she moved backward. "Will you wait?" she asked, still looking doubtfully at Gene.

Gene, appearing more poised and assured of herself than Carol had ever seen her, stepped into the foyer, Carol trailing her. The girl's eyes were wide. She had never *seen* such a hall! There was a make-believe tree in a shiny, daffodil-yellow wooden bucket. The floor was of tile set in wide black and white stripes, and the wall was literally covered with bold black and white pictures, all with yellow mats. A shiny black chair, with a daffodil-yellow cushion, stood primly by a table upon which was a post lantern. The foyer was gay. It was different. It was a proper introduction to the Burke living room.

After the maid departed, Gene moved on there, and Carol followed her; now both her eyes and her mouth were open. There were three steps down into the living room, carpeted, as was the foyer, in plushy, silvery gray. There were huge, deep chairs—great squares of blue-green luxury. There was a large picture of an armored horse hanging above a carved walnut chest. There was a low square table with books, two teacups in a heavenly blue, a tall white lamp with a green shade, a ceramic bowl of beautiful fruit. Real fruit. There was a round table with chairs set to either side of it, and an unfinished chess game, a pipe on a flat blue bowl. There was . . .

Gene touched her daughter's arm. "Don't stare," she murmured.

"But, *Mom*—" The chessmen were carved, white and black. The knights actually were knights, and the *bishop* . . .

At the far side of the room there was a flat blue door, centered with a yellow medallion. This door now opened, and through it came a man. A tall man, very thin, his shoulders somewhat stooped. His graying hair was combed back from a peak; he was magnificently attired in white tie and tails, and he carried a top hat in his hand. His eyes looked almost anxiously at the two women who waited.

Gene moved toward him. "Mike?" she said uncertainly.

"Oh, for Pete's sake!" He put the hat down on the table and came toward her quickly, his hands outstretched. He drew her to him and rested his cheek against her small hat. "Good heavens, Genie!" he cried. "How you have grown!"

Gene laughed and dabbed the finger of her white glove across her cheek. "Mike," she said, "this is Carol, my daughter."

Mike turned. "I am," he told the young girl, "definitely opposed to grown-up granddaughters. But—how are you, Carol?" He stooped and brushed her cheek with his lips.

Then he turned back to Gene with a dozen questions. He gestured at his formal garments. "This damned dinner," he protested. "I want only to talk to you—after all these years. But—look! Why don't you and Carol come with me?" He smiled charmingly at Carol. He was a completely engaging person, this young-looking grandfather.

He looks exactly like Gary Cooper, Carol would tell the girls at home. *But exactly!*

"Oh, we can't!" Gene was saying. "Mike, we can't!"

"Why can't you?"

Gene gestured to her dark-green linen dress and its green plaid coat. "Not to a gala dinner, Mike. I'll bet it's at the Waldorf!"

"Well, it is, of course, and there will be people dressed all ways—"

"Freaks."

"Of course." His deep-set eyes twinkled.

"I never relished being one of the freaks," said Gene emphatically.

"No-o. Well, look. If you don't have clothes with you . . ."

"We don't. Not that kind."

"But Addie has closets full of 'that kind.' You know she does. You could wear some of her duds—she wouldn't even recognize them. She's gone on—you know, for the reporters and photographers. I was going to stop for a drink or two, but now . . . You two go dress! And we'll go together. There's time, but hurry. *Scat!*"

Gene demurred a little, and Mike persuaded a little more. Carol was lost in a maze of fascinated disbelief. She was in a different world.

Mike won out. He summoned the maid—she was to assist his daughter and Miss Carol.

And Gene and Carol were going upstairs to Addie's bedroom and to the guest room across the hall.

Addie's bedroom was in green, a dark, velvety green, with a silvery painted bed, and a marble-topped table on which was set a silver tea service. There was a little fruitwood desk. One whole wall was of shuttered doors, behind which hung clothes—and clothes. Negligees, furs, and beautiful long-skirted concert gowns, beautiful short-skirted dinner gowns . . .

Gene made her selection, pushing the hangers about, dismissing the maid: "We won't need you. Carol, you take a quick shower."

The guest bathroom was Chinese red and ivory. The red towels were huge . . .

"I never was *in* such a place!" the girl gasped to her mother when she was ready for the white gown which Gene had selected. It was of some brocade material, made simply, the material draping and shining beautifully. There was a necklace of flat green stones, long white gloves, perfume.

Gene wrinkled her nose. "She always used too heavy perfume," she said. The dress she had chosen for herself was of creamy lace, with a vivid green cummerbund. Carol brushed her mother's hair and put her green necklace around Gene's throat.

"Just watch," Gene told the girl, "and try not to let those eyes pop out. I tried to tell you—"

"You couldn't tell me," said Carol. "I wouldn't have believed one word of it! The slippers pinch, Mom."

"Of course they do. Addie is smaller than we are. Can you stand it?"

"I will stand it."

The maid brought Gene a stole of green taffeta that matched the sash at her waist. There was a lacy shawl for Carol. The evening was warm.

They were ready. Gene looked at Carol, and they started down the stairs. "Don't show that you are frightened," Gene whispered.

"I'm not. Are you?"

"Petrified. Here's Mike."

Mike stood at the foot of the steps and watched them descend, his hand reaching to take Gene's, and he kissed her. "You look magnificent," he told his daughter. He turned then to Carol and stopped short.

The slender young girl in white, the light shining on her hair, her eyes eager—Mike Burke looked at her oddly and shook his head a little.

Gene put her hand on his arm. "She does look like Addie, doesn't she?" she asked. "I expect Carol is exactly what Addie was at nineteen."

Mike nodded, then coughed a little and took out his handkerchief. "I never saw Addie," he said, his voice muffled in the fine linen, "until she was past thirty."

"Well . . ." Gene moved on toward the front door, where the maid was waiting. "I expect we are late."

They were late. Very late. The car must thread its way through heavy traffic—stop, start, crawl, and stop again.

Then they finally entered the ballroom, a cineramic extravagance of crystal chandeliers, flowers, women in jewels and bright silks, the men counterpoints of black and white. There was red damask and gold leaf. The guests were seated at round tables throughout the room, and all heads were now turned toward the elevated head table, banked with flowers, where stood a distant, tiny figure in white, jewels agleam in her hair and on her hand as she talked and gestured.

Addie Burke was making a speech, graciously accepting the homage which had been paid her, the gifts . . .

She was like a figure in a marionette show, unreal, posturing and speaking. She was old. Even from this distance she looked old. Her voice came, plainly audible, through the microphones and amplifiers, but it was the voice of an old woman, a little high and shrill. Tremulous.

Gene looked long at Addie, then she turned and looked at Carol. The girl stood against the damask-paneled wall, under one of the silver-gilt sconces. She was not a pretty girl, but she had everything that Addie Burke would have considered the incomparable gift, better than jewels or awards—for

Carol was young, and fresh, and eager, with life before her.

Against her will, a lump rose in Gene's throat. She glanced at Mike. He too was looking from Addie to Carol and back again. Gene reached out her hand and touched his. He took her hand, drew her close, and smiled at her wryly.

"Tonight," Addie was saying, "you have given me the ultimate triumph. Now I can say that *life* has given me everything! Everything that a woman could ask of life, everything that I wanted, and dreamed of, as a child. Just hear the list!" In the spotlight her eyes glittered. "I have had romance," she cried. "Marriage, children, and professional success, crowned by tonight's wonderful, wonderful experience! Certainly that adds up to a full life for any woman!"

The toastmaster waited on the rolling, thundering applause. All over the room people were standing, cheering, applauding. Gene stared curiously at her mother. *Did* she think she had had a full life? Was she happy tonight? Yes. Because tonight's triumph was what passed for happiness for Addie Burke, and in its pleasure the rest could be forgotten.

The people sat down. The noise diminished, the applause ceased, and the toastmaster, a florid gentleman in a magnificent shirt front, was saying that only Addie Burke—"Only our dear Addie," the words rolled out fulsomely, "could have had such riches from life, because only Addie could be able, only Addie *was* able, to balance the claims of a family and a career without hurt to either one. She—"

Gene looked down at the floor and clenched her hands against her side.

Carol, wide-eyed, stared at the pageantry without understanding anything that was going on.

Michael Burke touched his daughter's arm. He could take no more of the admiration which the world was awarding its sentimental estimate of his wife's position. "Take me home, Gene," he said gruffly.

Gene turned and walked out through the silently opened

doors, down along the wide corridor. "To your home or mine, Mike?" she asked sensibly, when they had reached the elevators.

"That's no manner of a question," said Mike, gesturing to Carol to follow her mother. "I live in a cave. With vampire bats hanging from the ceiling."

Gene nodded. "We'll go change," she planned, in her usual, comfortable tones. "And you always will be welcome in my home, Father."

It was the first time she had ever called her young parent by that title. Now he smiled at her, and his shoulders straightened.

"I understand that I have more than one grandchild," he said, putting his hat on at a jaunty angle.

"Yes," said Gene. They must wait for his car. "I came to tell you about Shawn."

"I know about Shawn."

"You do? Has he written to you?"

"Last spring he came to me for help."

"But—"

"Yes. And now—it is too late. I—I have talked to the doctors. I—know about Shawn."

"Did you tell Addie?" asked Gene.

"Yes. She wouldn't believe it. She wouldn't listen."

Gene moved toward the advancing car. "I came to tell you about Shawn," she said again. "There is news about him. Good news."

"Oh?" Mike turned to look at her.

"The full report will be there when we get home."

"And it is good," said Mike.

"Yes."

Mike looked up at the great hotel, its lights, its flags. "It won't make much difference," he said thoughtfully. "Bad news didn't touch her. And good news won't matter, either. She lives in a shell, Genie."

"I know. But the rest of us—this is a second chance,

Mike."

"Yes," he said. "Yes. He and I—together. We'll make something of that chance."

The big car began to inch its way through traffic. It stopped, waited, pulled away again.

Carol smoothed the skirt of her beautiful white frock. "Are we going home *tonight,* Mom?" she asked wistfully.

"No," said Gene, with that sure dignity which she had acquired in this place, on this night. "I must stay to see Addie."

"My dear . . ." her father protested.

"I can do it," said Gene serenely. "Now I can talk to her. The old fears are gone, Mike. I have nothing left of the old resentment, either. But I have to see her."

"It may do no good."

"Perhaps not. But—I have to see her and talk to her."

Mike sat back in the car seat. "All right," he agreed. Then he straightened. "Look!" he said. "I'm afraid you think— I'm afraid that I gave you an idea—that I would desert Addie."

Gene shook her head. The jewels at her throat trembled and sparked fire. "Oh, no," she said firmly. "You wouldn't do that. Not after all these years. Not now."

"That's right. She's old, and she won't have her concerts. People forget . . .

"But I still mean to do for Shawn!" Mike spoke anxiously. "This second chance can't be lost."

"And of course you must visit your grandchildren, too," said Gene.

Mike answered her smile. "Certainly *that!*" he agreed. "Do you think I'll be a success with all these projects?"

Gene patted his hand.

Carol sat looking out at the lights, the people. "Mom," she said, in a tone of plaintive wonder, "don't you think we dressed up an awful lot to do nothing?"

Gene pressed her father's hand. "No," she said softly, "I think we dressed up a little bit to do a *lot!*"